TRAPPED

BY
MARIA HERNANDEZ

MCT Publications, LLC. :: New York

Trapped © 2010 by Maria Hernandez

MCT Publications, LLC
New York, New York

Printed in the United States of America

ISBN: 978-0-9979624-0-6

Artwork: Cure Art Studio, Miami, FL

Editor/Typesetter: Carla M. Dean, U Can Mark My Word

The Library of Congress has cataloged the soft cover edition as follows: Hernandez, Maria

Acknowledgments

First and foremost, I'd like to thank God, my mother Carmen Hernandez, and my brother Tommy Verdejo.

My family – Juan F. Lozada, cousin Jenny Rich and her son Bolivar Amil, my god-daughter Karen and her little ones Ciani and Salyna, my god-daughter Mahlet, my adopted god-daughter Nicole Noel, and the lovely Kathy Noel – My Comadre for life, my aunt Antonia Dalmau, my aunts, uncles and cousins from my Hernandez family, my late father Victor M. Hernandez.

My literary family – Author Sexy, CEO of Déjà vu Publications, who has shown me unconditional love and support from the moment we met, Author Donald Peebles, Author Carmen Noboa-Espinal, Author Tiffany Wright, Author Julie Ojeda-Nin, Author Erick S. Gray, Author K'wan, Author Adrian Ox Mendez, Nicolle Cure of Cure Art Studio in Miami FL. for her exciting ideas and designing my book cover, Carla M. Dean of U Can Mark My Word for working her wonderful magic with her editing of *Trapped* and her undying friendship, and to all the wonderful authors, editors, and friends who showed me love and served as great mentors.

I would also like to thank retired NYPD detective Norman Calderon for his expertise and guidance when I had many questions.

Last but certainly not least, I want to thank Author B. Jones, my inspiration.

To those not mentioned, please know you are in my heart and will be acknowledged in my second book.

TRAPPED

Prologue

11:00 p.m., West Harlem, NY

"Come on, Rosa. Hurry up and get your fat ass up those stairs," José whispered, while watching with lustful eyes as his girlfriend's ass jiggled with every step she took.

Rosa giggled and in a hushed tone replied, "I'm going as fast as I can. I don't want to make too much noise. You know Mami will kill me if she notices I'm not in my room."

"Well, it ain't my fault your mom decided not to go to work. It's like she knew I was back home. You didn't tell her I was being released, did you?" José asked.

"Hell no. She doesn't even know we're back together. She thinks I've given my heart to the Lord because I've been going to church, so she's trying to set me up with the pastor's son," she shared.

"A lot of good that'll do. Your horny ass could never be with a guy who thinks missionary position is the only way to satisfy you."

José grinned, then playfully smacked her backside.

Once on the rooftop, José quickly grabbed Rosa from behind and pushed her pajama bottoms down until they landed around her ankles. Eager to feel him inside her, she dropped to her hands and knees, and as soon as she was in position, José rammed his swollen manhood into her wet kitty. While his fingers rubbed her swollen clit, he slid his penis in and out of her vagina like a well-oiled piston. Waves of the orgasm building within her flowed through Rosa's young body, causing moans of ectasy to escape her lips and echo off the bricks of the rooftop.

"Ay, papi, just like that. Play with my pussy," she begged.

It didn't matter how long José went away, no other man made her feel the way he did.

Just as he was about to climax, the sound of the rooftop door slamming shut startled them.

"Damn it. Someone's watching us," José said, angered by the fact that he had slid his rod out of Rosa's warm vagina and fumble to pull up his jeans.

Rosa looked around nervously while adjusting her clothes.

"I hope it wasn't Mami."

"If it were your mom, she would've been cursing me in Spanish and trying to beat me up while I was fucking you. It must have been one of the neighborhood kids. Let me look over the edge and see what game they're playing."

Frustrated and annoyed, José stomped away to go look over the side of the building. He noticed a dark figure running out of the building's front entrance and towards 127th Street. The glare from the fluorescent lights below made it impossible to get a clear view of the person fleeing.

Suddenly, Rosa's piercing scream caused José to spin around in her direction.

"Oh my God! She's dead!"

He immediately rushed to where Rosa was standing over the bloody, lifeless body of a pretty young woman.

Chapter 1
Angelina Rivera

Angelina massaged her temples as she sat behind the wheel of her 1990 Mitsubishi Galant. She had finally made it home after a hard day's work and wanted to take advantage of the quiet time in her car. As the cool April breeze caressed her skin, she felt the tension slowly melt away from her body.

A forty-five-year-old single woman, Angelina had recently moved back to New York's East Harlem. While everyone looked forward to bringing in the year 2000, Angelina left the stable life she had built in Miami, Florida, and returned home. Looking around Taft Projects brought back a lot of memories, especially those of her parents, Victor and Ana. She could still hear her mother reminiscing about her crappy life on that side of town, a life all too familiar to Angelina.

Before meeting Victor, Ana and her mother moved to New York's El Barrio from Santurce, Puerto Rico, when Ana was nineteen years old. Ana's mother, Juana, rented a one-bedroom apartment on East 112th Street and Lexington Avenue. They knew little English but quickly adapted to life in El Barrio. Ana immediately found work at a hair net factory in New Jersey, and both women worked hard to survive.

Victor, on the other hand, came to the United States at the tender age of five when his family moved to the big city from

San Juan, Puerto Rico. His father, Arturo, had lost his first wife to cancer. After remarrying, Arturo moved his new wife and growing family to New York in search of the American dream. They soon learned there was no such thing. With Victor's younger siblings still in diapers, his stepmother stayed at home to care for them, which meant Arturo had to work several jobs in order to make ends meet. The stress of being the sole breadwinner soon started to weigh heavily on Arturo, and as a result, he turned to alcohol to escape the reality of his life. His heavy drinking took a toll on his family, who endured years of his abuse.

Ana and Victor met in the mid 1950's through mutual friends at a party in Harlem. It wasn't long before the two married and started a family of their own. In 1963, Taft Projects, located at 115th Street and Fifth Avenue, was a brand new development in El Barrio when Ana and Victor moved in. They saw the move as an opportunity to leave the cramped furnished room they had occupied for the past two years on the corner of Lexington Avenue and 117th Street and provide a better way of life for their three-month-old daughter, Angelina.

On the exterior, they seemed like a happy, stable family. Victor had a flourishing position in the maintenance department at the New York City Housing Authority, while Ana was a stay-at-home mom. What people didn't know was that their home was heavily strained by physical abuse and alcoholism. Apparently, when it came to Victor, the apple didn't fall far from the tree.

With her parents being raging alcoholics who fought constantly, Angelina's childhood was a turbulent one filled with heartache and disappointment. Shortly after Angelina's fourth birthday, the two finally separated. The divorce proceedings were just as volatile as their marriage. Once the judge awarded Ana full custody of Angelina, Victor turned his back on them, quit his job at the housing authority, and moved back to Puerto Rico, leaving them penniless. Unable to find work and on welfare, Ana found solace in liquor.

Angelina could still remember being five years old and cleaning up after her mother's booze parties. She would tiptoe into the living room to find her mother fast asleep on the couch, legs spread and drooling from the mouth. After quietly collecting the empty bottles of liquor and placing them in the trash, Angelina would retreat to her room to watch TV. She often cried herself to sleep, wondering why God had dealt her such a cruel hand and why her father didn't love her anymore. Her sadness turned to anger at the thought of having to clean up after her drunken mother every night. She had become her mother's caretaker at a very young age.

When Angelina walked into the apartment, she could hear her mother's bedroom television; the volume was set on the highest level. At seventy-nine years old, Ana's hearing was bad and she spent most of her time in bed watching her favorite Spanish soap operas. Gone were the days of endless parties at the Rivera household. Ana had suffered a heart attack ten years earlier, and her doctor warned her that smoking and drinking while taking her many medications did not mix. It was the wake-up call Angelina had been praying for. That day, Ana poured the contents of her last bottle of liquor down the drain and threw her remaining cigarettes in the trash. It was never too late to wipe the slate clean.

Placing her briefcase on the dining room table, Angelina decided to relax on the sofa before taking a shower. The soft cushions hugged her back as she rested her head on a small handmade pillow her grandmother had given her when she was a child. Her peace was interrupted by Ana's shriek.

"Angelina, come here for a second!"

"Damn, she doesn't give me a break," Angelina muttered to herself.

She slowly walked towards Ana's room. Once Angelina reached her mother's room, she leaned up against the doorframe to keep her tired body balanced.

"Yes, Mami?"

"Could you please go to the supermarket and get some things I need?" she asked.

Angelina felt the tension crawl up her spine. "Mami, how many times have I asked you to call me at work if you need anything? That way, I can get whatever you need before I get home."

"I'm sorry, mamita. I forgot to call you. You know I forget a lot of things," her mother answered with a pitiful look that expressed wanting forgiveness.

Her mother had been forgetting a lot of things lately, something that worried Angelina.

Angelina let out a long sigh while slowly shaking her head. "Okay, Mami. Make a list and I'll go to the supermarket."

When Ana suffered her heart attack, Angelica jumped on the first thing smoking out of Miami and was at her mother's side that evening. She looked at her mother's helpless body lying unconscious on the hospital bed and was overpowered by the fear of losing her. Despite all her faults, Ana never abandoned Angelina, unlike her deadbeat dad. Therefore, Angelina would not abandon her, either.

Angelina aimlessly walked up and down the supermarket aisles placing the requested items from her mother's shopping list into the cart. She smiled as she noticed the male clerks checking her out. Even dressed conservatively in her Liz Claiborne business suit, she was an eye-catching Latina for her age. Her daily workouts helped keep her 5'11" frame in shape and her soft DD breasts were still perky. Angelina's caramel-colored skin and jet-black, shoulder-length hair resembled that of a Taino Indian, and her big brown eyes drove men wild.

With the groceries loaded in the backseat, Angelina returned home. Turning onto 115th Street, she looked around for a good parking spot and noticed large headlights shining brightly in the dark not too far ahead. Quickly, she pressed on the gas and stopped nearby, ready to take the prized spot.

However, after a few minutes, she realized the car wasn't pulling out.

"Damn!" she cursed under her breath.

Noticing an empty spot next to the headlights, Angelina quickly positioned her car and backed into the narrow opening. Once she parked, she glanced through the passenger window and admired the glossy black Cadillac Escalade next to her. She also admired the fine-looking image draping his t-shirt over his tight wifebeater tee. Angelina couldn't help but stare at him. His arms were dark and muscular, and the diamond stud in his ear glistened as the rays from the streetlight illuminated the interior of his car.

Sensing her staring at him, he quickly turned his head and they made eye contact. Angelina's cheeks suddenly felt warm; she always blushed like a schoolgirl when she saw someone so pleasing to her eyes. Trying to hide her flushed cheeks, she quickly got out of the car and collected her belongings. He must have been racing to exit his vehicle, as well, because shortly after slamming the door shut, he immediately checked the pockets of his baggy jeans.

"Is everything okay?" Angelina asked as she placed her shopping bags on the sidewalk.

"No. It looks like I've locked my keys and cell phone in the truck," he answered.

Since it was her first time seeing him in the neighborhood, she figured he was a visitor.

"If you need to call someone, you can use my cell phone," she offered.

"That's alright. I live down the block at Foster Projects. Anyway, my mom taught me to keep a spare key in my wallet in case something like this happened," he responded with a grin.

As he reached for his wallet, she couldn't help but notice he wore his pants just below his firm, round butt, exposing his bright white boxers. There was a swagger about this brotha that somewhat turned her on.

13

She remained standing there until he gained access to his truck and was able to retrieve his keys and cell phone. Convinced he was okay, she picked up her shopping bags.

"Well, I gotta head home. Good night," Angelina said, then began walking away.

"Wait. Do you like reading books?" he asked.

She turned and walked back a few feet until she was standing in front of him. "Yeah. Why?"

"My name is Daryl James, and I wrote a book called *Betrayal*. It's the story of a man who becomes one of the biggest drug dealers in New York and is betrayed by the people he loves."

At first, Angelina seemed disinterested in the brief synopsis he shared. She had read many hood books and found them all to have the same backdrops consisting of drugs, sex, and violence. However, as he further explained the storyline, she became intrigued at how different his book was from the others. Curious, she placed her groceries on top of her car's trunk and reached in her purse.

"I'd like to read your book. How much?" she asked. "By the way, my name is Angelina."

"Pleasure to meet you, Angelina, and I sell the book for ten dollars," he answered with a pearly-white smile that captivated her. Then he shook her hand to seal the deal.

Daryl retrieved a copy of his book from the front seat of his truck and handed it to Angelina, who observed the cover. She was impressed by the professional design of the book cover; it had a necklace with a cross pendant draped over a gun and a stack of bills next to it. The word "Betrayal" was written in bold red letters above the image.

He began telling her of his past. Back then, he ran around the streets of Brooklyn selling crack. His high flying days ended when he and his partner sold five kilos of cocaine to an undercover cop. Daryl explained that he didn't feel comfortable with the sale; he had a feeling the buyer was a cop, but his partner assured him that the guy was okay. A few weeks prior, the mysterious buyer had established trust by becoming a regular customer, even buying a half a kilo at one point.

One night, Daryl and his partner met the undercover at an abandoned parking lot in Red Hook, Brooklyn, and everything changed. It was a big sale, one that would have both men on easy street for a long time. Once the deal had gone down, police vans and burly white guys sporting bulletproof vests suddenly surrounded Daryl and his partner. With their guns drawn, the officers warned them to get down on their stomachs and not move while they took control of the situation. That sale cost Daryl seven years in federal prison.

"The judge granted me a ten-thousand-dollar bond. I also needed letters of recommendation from friends and family, you know, to make sure I didn't flee the state. When I talked to my so-called homeboys and their families, they agreed to write the letters but it would cost me. I had to pay them three thousand dollars each. I needed to get out, so I asked my mom to give them the money in exchange for the letters. I was out in a week, but a year later, I was convicted and sent to Attica."

He paused long enough to light a cigarette.

"You know, Angelina, when I was hustling in the streets and the money was flowing, everyone wanted to be my friend and the honeys were all over me. As soon as I got caught, though, everyone turned their backs on me. My homeboys treated me like I had the plague, and the honeys started looking for the next best thing," he said, shaking his head.

As he spoke, Angelina couldn't help but respect him for trying to make it outside the drug game and build his own business.

"But, I learned my lesson," Daryl continued. "I'm gonna take care of those who take care of me."

"That's what's up," she said, while looking in her purse to see if she had enough cash on her to purchase his book.

After counting her money, Angelina shook her head in

15

disappointment. "Damn, I only have enough for tolls and lunch," she told him. "But, I get paid tomorrow and I'd really like to read your book. So, why don't we exchange phone numbers and I'll call you tomorrow evening?"

"Sounds like a plan," he replied.

They exchanged numbers and conversed for a bit more. As they talked, Angelina took a good look at him. He was the same height as her, with the muscular build of an African warrior. He kept his wavy hair short and diamond studs hugged his earlobes. His smooth skin was dark as night. He was no Denzel Washington, but his large brown eyes and pearly white teeth complemented his cute smile. His baggy jeans and crispy white Air Force Ones impressed her. Angelina always had a soft spot for a neatly dressed thug.

Angelina glanced at her watch and realized they had been talking for a little over an hour.

"Well, I gotta go home and get ready for work tomorrow." She extended her hand towards him. "I'll call you tomorrow evening, okay?"

Daryl shook her hand but didn't let go as he stared into her eyes. His look caused shockwaves of pleasure to rush through her veins.

"What I'd really like to do tomorrow is buy you a cup of coffee and talk some more, Angelina."

His touch and smooth voice ignited a flurry of sexual emotions she hadn't felt in a while.

"I would like that," she responded, trying hard not to stutter.

He smiled at her nervousness. He knew she was definitely interested.

"So it's on for tomorrow then. What time shall I pick you up?" he asked.

"Let's see, I get off work at five o'clock. So, you can pick me up in front of my building at seven. Is that time okay with you, Daryl?"

"Seven o'clock is a great time," he answered.

16

Daryl walked Angelina to the corner of 115th Street and 5th Avenue, where they exchanged goodbyes before he crossed the street and headed towards his residence. As she approached her building's entrance, a big smile spread across her face. That night, she fell asleep with Daryl on her mind.

Chapter 2
Daryl James

That night, Daryl lay in his small bedroom reflecting on how his life had changed in the last few months. Gone were the bars that held him captive seven long years. He could now relish the air conditioner that blew cool air into his room. He could eat, sleep, and even crap when he wanted to.

Feeling restless, he sat up on the side of the bed and stared at his reflection in the large mirror resting on his cherry oak dresser. His once youthful skin sported deep facial lines on his forehead and near the corners of his mouth. The abundant Afro he sported before his incarceration was now replaced by a short cut cleverly intended to disguise his receding hairline. At age thirty-eight, Daryl's life was filled with highs and lows most people twice his age had never experienced.

Born Daryl Agustus James at Cumberland Hospital in downtown Brooklyn, he was the apple of his mother's eye. Ramona gave birth to his older sibling Patrice four years earlier, but Patrice's father was awarded custody when Ramona's crack addiction got the better of her.

Daryl's dad, Tyrone, also lost his soul to the world of drugs, his drug of choice being heroine. Daryl was three months into this world when his father succumbed to the perils of the dark horse, dying when a syringe filled with pure "smack" plunged into his fragile veins and imploded his organs. They found him sitting on a filthy toilet and slumped over a vomit-filled sink in an abandoned building on Utica Avenue. He still had the belt tied around his frail arm and syringe inserted in his vein.

Tyrone's family wanted nothing to do with Ramona or Daryl, so Ramona had no choice but to enter a drug rehabilitation facility in Upstate New York, which housed women and their children. She later went through the "homeless system", living in a one-room space at Bethesda House of Upper New York, Inc. in the South Bronx and cooking on hotplates while caring for her baby boy. Six months of programs, classes, and applications paid off when Ramona was accepted into the Marcy Projects and placed in a two-bedroom apartment for her and her little one.

Ramona tried to raise her son with the hopes that he would become a great man. She made sure he attended school, enrolled him at the local Boys & Girls Club, and kept him busy with activities to steer his mind from the temptation to hustle. Yet, all her efforts proved to be to no avail. Daryl had the hustler's mentality in his blood, and at age ten, he became a mule for the local drug dealers who took over one of the empty apartments at the complex.

By the age of sixteen, he was selling crack on his own. At first, Ramona complained about how she didn't want her child selling the same drug that almost destroyed her life, but her attitude quickly changed when she came home from work one day and found new furniture adorning her apartment. That same day, Ramona was further surprised with a Louis Vuitton handbag she'd had her eye on for some time. All of the good morals she tried to instill in her son went out the window.

When Daryl's illegal dealings finally caught up with him and he was sent away, Ramona figured she had to start a new life without her son. The money wasn't rolling in and she grew tired of the gossip surrounding her. The last straw came when the housing manager informed her that she would be moved to a studio apartment in Staten Island since Daryl, now a convicted felon, could not remain on the lease.

It was then that she got the idea to become a foster mother. She had no prior arrests, and by accepting foster children, she knew they would allow her to stay in a larger apartment. She endured six months of counselors, home inspections, and psychiatric evaluations before finally being awarded three toddlers from different families. Six months later, she was transferred to a three-bedroom apartment at Foster Projects in West Harlem. Upon Daryl's release, she immediately shuffled the kids to one bedroom and prepared the larger bedroom for Daryl...her flesh and blood, her one true son, the one who would make everything all right again.

While in prison, Daryl proved to be an exemplary inmate. He took writing classes and held down a job. The more he wrote, the more he found peace in words and discovered a talent for writing stories. Ultimately, he began penning a book, and by the time he was released from prison, he was a self-published author ready to change his life.

*****

Early the next morning, Daryl set out on his grind. His destination? Fulton Mall, where street vendors lined the sidewalks of Fulton Avenue selling hood books alongside various clothing stores. Turning on his street charm, he got some vendors to buy his book on the spot while others promised to place their orders over the weekend.

A few hours later, he walked towards his truck and noticed Butta Face coming up the block. Her birthname was Sandra Anderson, but everyone knew her by her nickname.

At a young age, Sandra had dreams of becoming a nurse and worked hard at being a straight "A" student in school. She wanted to break free of her drug-infested neighborhood as well as her cocaine-addicted mother, who not only smoked it but did everything possible to get it. Sandra's mother discovered the easiest way to support her habit was to sell her body.

Sandra would slowly walk up the steps to the fifth floor apartment she shared with her mother on Keap and Grand Street in the Williamsburg section of Brooklyn. Recognizing the all too familiar smell of marijuana and crack seeping from underneath the door, Sandra would walk straight into her bedroom while trying to ignore the erotic moans coming from the living room. There was no shame in her mother's game. One day, Sandra walked in to find her mother with two white men dressed in Con Edison uniforms. One man was standing over her, enjoying how his pink manhood disappeared into her mother's mouth while the other man rammed his rod into her rectum with no mercy.

By age fifteen, Sandra grew tired of wearing the same old clothes from the Goodwill since her mother spent all of the money welfare provided on her drug habit. She wanted to dress in nice clothes like the other girls in her neighborhood. So, she decided to drop out of school and follow in her mother's footsteps, using her kitty in exchange for goods.

She only flirted with men that she knew had money and soon had her own customers making visits to her bedroom. They paid good amounts of money for a chance to be with a young girl. Dropping her birth name, she became Butta Face and adopted her favorite phrase, "Crack is whack, but a Gucci bag is forever!"

"Yo, Butta! Let me holla at ya for a sec!" Daryl shouted as he walked around the back of his truck.

Her eyes glistened at the delightful sound of Daryl's voice. Butta Face had a crush on Daryl from the moment she saw him hanging out with his boys at the corner store. She was a skinny fourteen-year-old at the time with pigtails and braces. Butta Face was mesmerized at how his homeboys hung on the seventeen-year-old's every word as though he was a god. Her panties would always get wet at the mere thought of Daryl's tool in her kitty.

At five feet tall and 180 pounds, Butta Face didn't fit the

petite criteria of most hoodrats, but her DD breasts and fat booty appealed to most men looking for a quick lay. Her overall persona left little to be desired. Her skin was lighter than most black chicks, and her thin, light brown hair fell to the sides of her face. Her crooked smile and lips were way too plump for her small face, and her pug nose resembled a shriveled pimento. This day, Butta Face was dressed in a pair of casual jeans two sizes smaller than her actual size; the black pullover she wore was tight enough to reveal her plump love handles and fatty arms.

"Hey, Daryl, what's good?" she said while strutting towards him.

"Here on my grind. You know how it is. Did you read my book yet?" he asked, flashing a devilish grin.

"Yes, I did. I stayed up all night reading it! Thanks for signing it for me," she answered seductively.

Daryl smiled as he hungrily checked her out like a lion inspecting its prey. He made it a point to give a copy of his book to all the little chickenheads he came across. He signed it so they would feel special. The inscription was always the same: "To the most beautiful woman in Brooklyn; from your favorite writer, Daryl James." Honestly, Daryl didn't give a damn about them or Butta Face. He just wanted to make sure the book kept circulating, knowing the little bitches were the best free advertisement he could get.

He got close to Butta Face and grabbed her huge ass.

"How about you show daddy how much you loved his book? Do you have time to go to a telly?" he asked with a smug smile.

"Yes, daddy, I do," she answered softly.

With no further words, they quickly hopped into his truck and drove off.

Crossing over the Manhattan Bridge, they made their way to a cheap motel on 152nd Street and St. Nicholas Avenue. He would have stayed out in Brooklyn, but he wanted to be close to home. Knowing Butta Face and her mother moved to 140th

23

Street and Lenox Avenue a few years ago, he knew he wouldn't have to drive far to drop her ass off afterwards.

As soon as they stepped into the room, Butta Face tore her clothes off so quickly one would have thought they were on fire. It didn't take long for Daryl to have her on all fours and ramming his huge manhood into her kitty. Butta Face proved to be just as much of a freak as he was. She aggressively pushed him onto his back, climbed on top of him, and rode him like a prized stallion.

"Oh, daddy! I love riding you!" she yelled, moving her hips faster and harder.

Grunting, Daryl grabbed her hips and thrusted so deep inside of her that he swore he could feel her ovaries. She experienced pain between her walls with each stroke, but she didn't care. Only thing she was concerned about was getting hers.

Daryl felt his sack rumble and knew he was about to explode.

"Suck my dick!" he grunted, then pushed her off him and aimed her crooked mouth to his dark horse.

She sucked on him like a hungry animal; up and down his shaft her mouth went. Grabbing the back of her head, he shoved his dark horse deep down her throat. Butta Face gagged so hard she almost threw up. After a few more strokes, he shot his creamy load in her mouth, almost choking her to death.

Once Daryl finished shooting his load, Butta Face rolled over on her back and tried to catch her breath as she swallowed the last of his juice. Without saying a word, Daryl immediately got up and headed to the bathroom to clean himself.

The bathroom at the motel was standard size and complete with two small bars of soap, the kind that would instantly dry out a person's skin. The towels hanging over the rusty rack hadn't seen fabric softener in ages, and the plastic curtains of the shower stall had seen better days. Daryl

24

adjusted the rusty knobs until the water reached the temperature he liked. Then he removed the wrapper from the tiny bar of soap and began lathering his aching sack. Making his way up to his chest, he felt relief as the hot water trickled over his smooth skin. Just as he was feeling like his old self, he heard the shower curtain being pulled back and in stepped Butta Face. Disgusted, he quickly got out and began drying off.

"Baby, where you going? I wanted to wash your back," she whined.

He didn't answer. Instead, he wrapped the coarse towel around his waist and went into the other room where he quickly got dressed. After making sure his rings and Jesus piece were in place, he was ready to go. He glanced towards the bathroom where Butta Face was still showering.

"Yo, hurry the fuck up! I got things to do," he yelled.

Daryl felt his luck had finally changed when he found himself in a deep conversation with the hot Latina he met last night. Thoughts of Angelina came into play. There was something about her that he liked, and he planned to get to know her better.

There's something different about this woman. Let's see how tonight turns out, he thought, while staring at her number saved in his cell phone.

Chapter 3
Rollercoaster Ride

The Grand Central Parkway was a nightmare. Driving through Long Island was the usual breeze; however, traffic was at a standstill the closer Angelina got to LaGuardia Airport. It seemed like everyone was coming in or leaving out of New York. Frustrated, she banged her fist on the steering wheel.

"Dammit! I'm gonna be late."

Angelina had spent the day checking the time on her computer in anticipation of her date with Daryl. The mortgage company she worked for in Hempstead, New York, was as crazy as ever that particular Friday. Loan officers crowded around her desk, stressing her and wanting answers to make sure their loans went through before they left. Angelina was ready to send them all to hell. The job of a mortgage processor wasn't a glamorous one. One moment, they loved her, and the next moment, they wanted to have her head if their loan didn't go through. The plus side about her occupation was the good salary. Anglelina had been in the same profession for many years; therefore, she knew her craft well. As crazy as the workday had been, time seemed to move too slowly for her liking. She wanted to get home in time for her coffee date with Daryl.

Miraculously, traffic cleared once she passed the airport. So, she was able to breeze across the Triboro Bridge and get home in less than twenty minutes. Once home, Angelina frantically unlocked the front door and made her way down the narrow hallway of her mother's apartment. She stopped at the doorway of her mother's bedroom to smile at the sight of Ana lying comfortably on her bed watching her favorite Spanish game show. Ana took her eyes off the TV long enough to smile up at Angelina.

"Hi, Mamita. I made arroz con pollo with roasted chicken. Are you hungry?"

"No, Mami. I'm going out with a friend," Angelina replied, then hurried to her bedroom.

"And who is this friend?" Ana asked, lowering the TV's volume so she could hear her daughter's reply.

"She's a friend from high school," Angelina lied.

Before Ana had a chance to continue her interrogation, Angelina closed the door behind her.

Flipping through the clothes hanging in her closet, Angelina decided to wear her turquoise Coogie halter blouse with a pair of black Coogie jeans. The blouse tied at the neck and showed off her silky-soft shoulders, and its loose fit below her breasts would cover any imperfections. For her footwear, she chose her black and grey Coach sandals, pairing it with her matching Coach clutch purse. Once satisfied with her selections, she grabbed her terrycloth robe and headed towards the bathroom to take a shower.

Once she finished showering and getting dressed, Angelina stood in front of the bathroom mirror to apply her makeup, but the ringing of her cell phone interrupted her. It was 6:55 p.m. She smiled upon recognizing the voice on the other end.

"This is Daryl James, author of *Betrayal*, the hottest book on the planet," he said jokingly.

Angelina giggled. "Hi, Daryl. What's good?"

"It's all good now that I'm talking to you. Listen, I'm leaving my house in five minutes. I'll call you when I'm in front of your building."

"Perfect. I'm almost ready myself," she told him. "See you soon."

Angelina finished applying her makeup, then stepped back to carefully inspect her outfit and hair in the full-length mirror hanging on the closet door. Opting to tie the top part of her hair at the crown, her lower locks flowed over her shoulders and back.

As she reached to grab her purse, the phone rang again.

"Hey, Angelina, I'm downstairs."

"Perfect timing; I'm heading downstairs now," she answered.

Angelina entered her mother's bedroom, gently kissed her on the forehead, and out the door she went. Upon stepping outside, she saw Daryl smoking a Newport cigarette while leaning against his driver's side door. He was dressed casually, wearing a loose-fitting red t-shirt and black jeans with black and red Nike sneakers.

"Hello, Mr. James." She greeted him formally as she made her way towards him, yet she felt totally comfortable in his presence.

"Hello, Ms. Rivera. You look great," he answered, his eyes admiring her image.

Angelina was impressed by how Daryl walked with her to the passenger side of the Escalade and opened the door to let her in. *Such a gentleman,* she thought to herself as she slid onto the seat. He even helped her with fastening the seatbelt. Daryl had an excellent collection of CDs that included sweet R&B classics by Al B. Sure, SWV, and Gerald Levert. The soft, intoxicating sounds coming from the speakers serenaded her as they drove down Fifth Avenue.

"Is it alright if I stop by the printer to pick up some custom t-shirts I ordered?" he asked.

"I don't mind at all," Angelina replied.

The print shop was located on Lenox Avenue between 123rd and 124th Streets. Angelina noticed the crowd of customers inside the store as Daryl parked.

"Don't let the crowd worry you. The clerk has my order ready. It should take no more than ten minutes," Daryl said, then reached over and gently squeezed her hand.

As Daryl made his way into the store, Angelina couldn't help but watch him. He walked with the confidence of a man on a misson, a misson to become a well-known writer. She imagined herself by his side enjoying the ride.

Daryl exited the print shop carrying a cardboard box filled with red t-shirts that showcased his book cover. He placed them on the backseat before sliding behind the steering wheel.

While adjusting his seatbelt, he gazed at Angelina with a look of curiosity.

"Can I ask you a question?"

"Sure," she replied without a care.

"I'm just curious to know why a girl as fine as yourself is single?"

Angelina was taken aback by the question. She didn't think he would get so personal so soon.

"Well, I can assure you it's not because I'm some psycho chick," she replied with a smile.

Sensing he crossed the line, he softened his tone.

"I know you're not a psycho. Trust me, I can tell those types a mile away. I'm just curious because you seem like a woman who has her life together, but I also sense you haven't found the right guy who will treat you like the queen I know you are."

His question made Angelina a little apprehensive. She wasn't ready to pour her heart out to someone she had just met; she also didn't want to say the wrong thing and scare him off. Truth is, although Angelina was a beautiful woman, she suffered from very low self-esteem that stemmed from her childhood. Being the tallest child in her class didn't make her very popular, and the men she loved never stayed. However, there was something about the way he looked at her that made her feel comfortable.

"Well, I'll tell you a bit of my history. I've been married twice in my lifetime. I was young and stupid the first time I married, and the second time, I was just stupid."

They both chuckled at her statement.

Feeling more at ease, Angelina continued, "Juan and I were together from the age of fifteen, married at nineteen. He cheated on me from day one until our divorce three years later. In my mid-twenties, I met and married my second husband, Raul. He was a widower with two daughters. At that time, I was at the stage of my life where I wanted to be a wife and mother. Six years later, he fell in love with someone else. So, we divorced and I haven't seen him or his daughters since. You see, I'm the type of woman who wears her heart on her sleeve. When I love someone, it's for real. I pour my heart and soul into the relationship and always end up with the short end of the stick. That's why I prefer to stay alone."

Angelina felt a slight pain in her chest as she made that statement. It was the first time she had talked about her personal failures with anyone except her cousin Jennie.

Daryl shook his head. "It's a shame, 'cause you're not only pretty but smart as hell."

"I survived," Angelina replied, shrugging her shoulders.

Sensing her pain, Daryl leaned over and softly brushed his hand against her cheek.

"I wish I would've met you seven years ago. You sound like a woman who rolls with her man no matter what. Those bitch-ass niggas didn't appreciate you, but I promise you once we get to know each other, I'll show you that I'm nothing like them."

Angelina wanted to believe him, but experience had taught her to be more careful.

"So how about we get that coffee?" she asked, desperately wanting to change the subject.

Daryl leaned back and chuckled. "Listen, I don't want to lie to you on our first date, so I have to confess something. I don't drink coffee."

She, too, leaned back and smiled. "Well then, I must confess something, as well. I only drink coffee in the morning, and my stomach is so twisted right now I couldn't stomach a large meal."

There was a short silence inside the truck followed by hearty laughs from Daryl and Angelina.

"Okay, Ms. Rivera, do you know of a good pizza spot?" he asked as he slid the key in the ignition.

"Oh yeah, the best pizza in East Harlem is at 116th Street and Lexington Avenue, right by the train station…Sam's Famous Pizza," she answered.

They arrived at the pizza spot and ordered two slices of pizza along with two cans of Sprite. Opting to eat inside his truck, Daryl drove back to 115th Street, parking at a nice spot between Madison and Fifth Avenue. They ate their pizza and talked more freely. Angelina's ribs felt like they were about to crack as Daryl entertained her with his off-the-wall jokes. She hadn't had that much fun in a long time, and Daryl made sure to hold her interest. Laughing so much left her a bit weak, so she leaned towards him and rested her head on his broad shoulder.

Daryl boldly yet gently held her chin and brushed his lips against hers. Suddenly, his full lips devoured her eager mouth as their tongues met. Her body tingled with desire; she yearned for Daryl's manhood to be inside her. Daryl's hand gently caressed her shoulder, then expertly made its way over her chest to her breast. Massaging her right mound, he gently pinched her nipple through her blouse, causing her to draw back a bit but not enough to pull away. It was a moment where they didn't care what was going on around them; it was as if they were the only human beings on earth.

As Daryl glanced at his car stereo, he stiffened before gently pushing Angelina away.

"What's the matter?" she asked, breathless.

"It's not you, baby. God knows I want you. I need to be honest with you. I'm on parole and have to be at home by nine o'clock."

Angelina checked her watch and noticed it was 8:45 p.m. By the look on his face, Angelina could sense he was feeling a bit embarrassed about his curfew.

"Tell you what, why don't we meet tomorrow morning for breakfast and we'll pick up where we left off?" he said softly.

She gently caressed his chest. "That sounds like a good idea. I wouldn't want to see you get in any trouble."

Angelina caressed his muscular arms, then boldly let her hand travel down to his pants. When she felt his stiff manhood, she couldn't believe how huge he was, making her want him even more.

Angelina, you're gonna get tore up, she thought to herself as she continued exploring him. The thought of him inside her ignited her desire.

Daryl suddenly reached over, turned the ignition key, and started his truck.

"Where are we going?" Angelina asked, confused.

"We're gonna have breakfast," he answered as he put the truck in drive and pulled out of the parking spot.

Daryl and Angelina's destination was a quaint, out-of-the-way motel on the Bronx side of the Whitestone Bridge. As soon as he locked the motel room door, the clothes flew off their bodies, their naked flesh entangled on the queen-sized bed, and they went at each other like hungry beasts.

The sex was amazing! Daryl and Angelina had sex in every position known to humans and a couple of positions Angelina didn't even know existed. When his manhood entered her waiting canal, he knew by her tightness she hadn't been with anyone else in quite some time. Angelina couldn't believe how tight she was either, but once her lust juices started flowing, she felt more relaxed and melted into him. Daryl thrusted his tool inside her deep and hard, leaving her breathless. With every thrust, Angelina let out moans of pain and pleasure.

At one point, they made their way to the shower. His skin felt so smooth that Angelina couldn't help but gently kiss his shoulders and back as she reached around him from behind and began rubbing his massive tool. Soon after, his erection returned. He gently positioned his body behind her and started kissing her on the back of her neck while his hands caressed her aching breasts. They found themselves making love in the shower as the warm water trickled down their bodies.

It was 1:30 a.m. when they dressed and readied for their trip back home, exhausted from their sexcapade. Daryl sat on the edge of the bed watching Angelina as she stood in front of the dresser mirror and adjusted her earrings. Being with her brought warm feelings he had never experienced.

"Angelina, I just want you to know I really like you, and I would love to get to know you," he said softly.

On the outside, Angelina kept her composure, but inside, she was as happy as a schoolgirl kissing her first crush.

She leaned on the dresser and with a smile replied, "I would like that."

Chapter 4
Lustful Honeymoon

The months that followed were magical. Daryl let Angelina into his world as he navigated through the urban publishing business. His book was the talk of the town, receiving rave reviews from book clubs and readers.

At the same time, the mortgage industry started drying up. Interest rates were sky high. Many loan officers resorted to unscrupulous ways of tricking unsuspecting homebuyers into purchasing homes at two-year low-fixed rates, telling them that they would be able to refinance before their rate ballooned to three times their original one with the same rate at the time of closing. What many didn't know was once they signed on the dotted line, they were stuck with the loan for five years before they could refinance. Many families wound up foreclosing on their homes from being misled.

Angelina didn't like misleading people, and as a result, she was terminated from her position when the supervisors found out she was telling prospective buyers the truth. Fearing she would go to the authorities with what she knew, Angelina was given a generous severance pay and told she could apply for unemployment. Being a smart cookie afforded her to have a nice amount of savings in her bank account from her bonuses and recently acquired funds from her dismissal.

Instead of being discouraged by the fact that she had lost her job, she saw it as an opportunity to spend more time with

Daryl. Their relationship grew as they spent their days getting his publishing company in order and their nights enraptured in passionate lovemaking.

However, while Angelina thought she had finally found the man of her dreams, Daryl began to see her as his moneymaker. The more he got to know her, the more he learned how knowledgeable she was when it came to business, something Daryl was not familiar with handling. Sure, he knew what to do when it came to the drug game, but when dealing with legitimate business people, he didn't have the patience or savviness that Angelina possessed. Daryl knew the more responsibilities he gave her, the better the chances of his book sales rising.

Angelina, on the other hand, viewed Daryl as her knight in shining armor. He did everything possible to make her feel special, something she had yearned for as long as she could remember. She saw his confidence in her as a sign of his love. Angelina figured if he was comfortable trusting her with his professional affairs, it meant he loved her. Angelina soon found herself dreaming of spending the rest of her life with him. She would stand by his side during his journey to become one of the greatest authors of all time. She often fantasized about the two of them ten years into the future, raising his daughter and living happily ever after in a cozy home.

For the first month following their first date, Angelina promised herself to observe Daryl before commiting to him. Her past experiences had been painful, and she had the worst track record when it came to men. First, her father Victor–a man she could still remember loving with all her heart–left and never looked for his only daughter again, followed by a string of relationships that ended in failure. But, love took over as she decided to throw caution to the wind.

A few months before meeting Daryl, Angelina had decided to see a therapist, who came to the conclusion that because of her father's abandonment, Angelina sought acceptance from the men who cheated on and hurt her, and she did so in fear of being abandoned again. Angelina thought the therapist was the one who was crazy. She hated her dad for leaving her, so why would she be looking for someone similar to replace him?

What the therapist's sessions did discover was that she had two personalities: Angelina and Tutie. Angelina fit into the therapist's mold. She was the one who cried every night for the first year after her father left and who thought the only way to keep a man was to submit to his every whim, only to be disappointed when they would leave her without an explanation. Tutie would be the one who would take over when Angelina was in too much pain; she was the bitch who pushed all of those feelings to the side in order to rid herself of the pain she endured.

Once Angelina met someone she thought was special, she would put Tutie's personality to sleep instead of letting her continue to observe him; Angelina was scared Tutie would push Daryl away, not realizing her weaker alter ego was the one doing the pushing. The first month into their relationship, Tutie observed Daryl's wine-and-dine attitude with scrutiny. However, as Daryl kept pouring on his charm, Angelina awoke, and convinced that he was the one, she quickly placed Tutie into what could be considered an induced coma.

Soon, Mo' Money Publication was the buzz of New York as well as their relationship. She was his accountant, marketing manager, sales representative, shipper, and negotiator. You name it, Angelina was it. Working long hours for the publishing company proved to be a challenge for her, but she didn't care. As far as she was concerned, Daryl would be with her forever. So, they were a team.

Daryl's book circulated well throughout the five boroughs, but his big break came when he was asked to attend a book signing in Philadelphia, Pennsylvania. Philadelphia was considered to have the largest number of readers in the northeast, and they knew if his book did well there, *Betrayal* would be a hit all over the United States.

At seven o'clock the morning of the signing, they headed out to Philly. Leaving early would allow them to stop for breakfast and give them plenty of traveling time in case they ran into traffic along the way. As they were riding on the New Jersey Turnpike listening to the radio, excitement overcame Daryl.

"Baby, if this book signing is a success, there will be no stopping me," he blurted out.

"That's right, baby. You will be a success," she replied proudly.

"No, *WE* will be a success. You've helped me so much, Angelina. If it weren't for your help, I'd still be peddling my book on street corners. You're one smart woman, babe."

His words touched her heart.

"Well, I just hope your ass won't leave me for some super model when you make it big time," she joked.

Daryl laughed. "Naw. Those bitches are too damn skinny anyway. Not my type." His voice took on a serious tone. "Plus, I have a good woman sitting right next to me. You've been there for me, babe, and I wouldn't throw dirt on you like that."

"You know, I'm starting to feel confident that you won't," she answered as she caressed his arm.

He placed his free hand on her thigh and caressed the inner area next to her coochie, igniting her lustful fire.

"Baby, I wanna make love to you right now," he said in his husky voice.

"But you're driving, and we don't have time to find a motel," Angelina replied.

"So why don't you come over here and give Daddy some good loving with that mouth of yours. You know that's what you like doing."

Daryl removed his hand from her thigh and started undoing his belt buckle. He knew her all too well. Angelina loved licking his large Tootsie Roll as much as he loved watching her do it.

Angelina didn't waste any time grabbing his massive tool with both hands, taking him on as he drove down the turnpike. Her thong was moist with love juices as her sensuous lips stroked his hard-on in a rhythmic pace. Daryl brought out the freak in her. She didn't care where they got freaky as long as they did.

Daryl couldn't take it anymore. Angelina's mouth felt smooth on his shaft and he wanted her right then and there. Noticing an empty rest stop up ahead, he made his way to the exit and parked at a spot that had long tree branches hanging overhead, the perfect hiding place. When he stopped the vehicle, Angelina sat up.

"Where are we?" she asked, looking around suspiciously.

"I gotta take care of my boo, too. Let's go to the backseat," he said softly.

She quickly slid in between the front seats and was soon relaxing in the back. With their clothes off, Daryl thrust his throbbing rod deep inside her, causing the Escalade to rock back and forth with their movements.

"Baby, I'm all yours," she whispered, while digging her long fingernails into the skin on his back.

"You're all *mine*?" he asked, thrusting deeper inside of her.

"Yes, papi, I am," she replied in delight.

It was exactly what he wanted to hear. Daryl buried his head in her neck and continued to move at a furious pace. He felt the fire growing in his sack, a sign he was about to explode.

"Baby, I'm about to burst!" he yelled.

Within a few seconds, he shot his warm load inside her. She loved the look of satisfaction on his face as his body trembled. Exhausted, he lay on top of her, running his fingers through her long locs.

Once they recovered from the intense lovemaking, they sat up and began gathering their clothes from the car floor.

"Baby, when we get back from Philly, I want you to stay at my mom's house, okay? I wanna feel you next to me all night," he said as he gave her a clean paper towel to wipe herself.

"Okay, love, but let's hurry and get dressed so we can get to the book signing. Last thing we need is to get arrested for getting busy on the side of the highway," she replied jokingly.

They arrived in Philly by eleven o'clock. The bookstore was located on the lower level of Philadelphia's largest mall on Market Street. Tamara, the owner of Sunset Book Store, warmly greeted them. She was thirty-two years old, stood 5'2", and a bit chunky, but not to the point of being fat. She wore her dark brown hair pulled back, revealing her soft caramel-colored skin. Recognizing Daryl when he entered, she smiled as she made her way around the counter and walked towards him. The two had met a few weeks earlier when he visited her flagship store in Queens and they hit it off immediately.

"Hey, you made it! Was the drive difficult?" Tamara asked.

"No, it wasn't. We would've been here sooner, but we stopped for breakfast," he said as he lovingly winked at Angelina, making her blush. "Let me introduce you to Angelina Rivera, my marketing manager," Daryl continued, wrapping his arm around Angelina's waist.

Angelina liked the sound of that. She didn't know what title to give herself and was happy Daryl could think so quickly. Switching to professional mode, she extended her hand toward Tamara.

"Nice to meet you," she said with a firm handshake.

"Same here, my dear. Daryl has told me of you. He's told me that you have helped him so much," Tamara said with enthusiasm.

"I've done what I could," Angelina replied modestly.

"No, you've done a lot, babe," Daryl stated.

Tamara raised her eyebrows. "Babe? So I take it you're

more than his manager, huh?" she stated jokingly with a wink.

"This is my boo," Daryl answered, his tone expressing pride.

"Well, you two make a fine couple," Tamara complimented.

Angelina felt good hearing her flattering remark. Their nine-year age difference was a sticky point for her, mainly because she didn't want Daryl to feel embarrassed by the fact that she was older. He always assured her that age was nothing but a number, and it didn't bother him. "If anyone has a problem with it, fuck it. They don't do for me what you do," he would tell her.

Tamara pointed towards the table located by the entrance.

"Well, as you can see, I already got the table set up. It's early, so it'll be a little slow. But, after one o'clock, people will start coming in."

"Okay. We'll go to the car and get the books. Do you still want me to bring in the amount of books we agreed on?" he asked.

"Definitely! Let's get this started," Tamara said as she clapped her hands together once.

Tamara was right. Around quarter after one, things picked up and the customers started pouring in. Daryl kept busy autographing his books and talking with his new fans. He was on fire! Angelina captured the moments on her cell phone so Daryl could display the pictures of him with his fans on his website. There were a lot of females eager to take a picture with him and many young things flirting, as well. Angelina just laughed. They could flirt with him all they liked, because she knew at the end of the day he'd be going home with her.

Later that day, Angelina decided to leave Daryl to the business of his book signing and tour the mall. She walked into different stores and struck up conversations with the customers who admired her red t-shirt advertising Daryl's book. She took the opportunity to let them know the author was in the area signing his book. When she returned to the bookstore, the seventy or so people waiting on line to get an autographed copy let her know she had done a good job at promoting her baby's book.

By four o'clock, Daryl decided to pack up and head back to New York. Realizing they hadn't eaten at all that day, Daryl and Angelina decided to first stop at a local fast food restaurant before hitting the road.

"Boo, I made fifteen hundred dollars this book signing, and their bookstore in Queens wants another five hundred copies," he told her as they sat by the full-lenth window that overlooked the mall.

"Wow, baby! That's great!" she said.

"Yes, it is. Tamara loved the event so much that she wants me to come by next month for another signing," he said, then shook his hand that had started to cramp. "My hand hurts from all that signing, though."

Angelina laughed. "Poor, baby. When we get back home, I'll take care of it, okay?"

"You'll take care of my hand and everything else, right?" he asked, his tone filled with lust.

Angelina giggled. "Yes, baby, I'll take care of all that ails you."

The ride back home wasn't as smooth as when they were driving to the book signing. The light rain shower that began in Philadelphia turned into a downpour as they approached New York City, and the Holland Tunnel was backed up with traffic as usual. Despite those things, they were able to make it to their destination before his curfew.

When they arrived at his mother's apartment, they found Ramona sitting on the sofa watching her favorite detective show. She had grown fond of Angelina and was happy Daryl had met a woman to guide him down the right path. Of all the women she met, Ramona saw Angelina as someone who would keep her son on the straight and narrow, just as she felt with his baby's mother at one time.

Angelina bent over and kissed Ramona on her cheek.

"Hi, Ramona, how are you feeling today?"

"I'm fine, love. How did it go in Philly?" Ramona asked.

"It went great, Mommy. My hand hurts from all that signing."

Suddenly, Angelina could see the little boy in him as he stood there pouting while massaging his hand.

"You need to soak your hand in cold water, baby. Did you two eat?" Ramona asked.

"Yes, we did, but I'm so tired. I just wanna take a shower and hit the sack," Angelina replied.

"Well, go ahead and make yourself comfortable. You know this is your house, too," Ramona told her.

Ramona always went out of her way to make Angelina feel welcome. From the moment they met, Angelina looked at her as a second mother.

"Thanks, Ramona," Angelina said with a warm smile before heading towards Daryl's room.

Too exhausted from the day's events, any thoughts Daryl and Angelina had of making love went out the window. Instead, they showered, climbed into Daryl's bed, and fell into a blissful sleep.

Chapter 5
Temptation Hits Home

It was the second Sunday of July and the day of the Harlem Book Fair. Urban authors from the tri-state area as well as from other states gathered on 135th Street from Lenox Avenue to Eighth Avenue to showcase their releases. Angelina tried to convince Daryl to rent a table, but he thought it would be a waste of time. Lately, he had been dissatisfied with the lack of funds flowing into his new legitimate business but loved the attention from the groupies, which inspired him to work on part two of his book.

With his newfound success, Daryl became bored with Angelina. Daryl missed the old days when he hustled his crack and had a different woman every night. The only other woman he tried to settle down with was his baby's mama, Katrina. They met one summer when Ramona sent him to Tallahassee, Florida, in her many attempts to keep him off the streets. He was seventeen years old and fell hard for the young preacher's daughter when his church-fearing aunt forced him to attend church with her. Katrina was a sixteen-year-old luscious redbone with thick hips and huge breasts. Her green eyes were hypnotic and could bring any man to his knees; he wanted her in the worst way.

Utilizing his skill of seduction, Daryl persuaded Katrina into letting him sneak into her room where she surrendered herself to him, losing her virginity as they made passionate love. They spent the entire summer quenching each other's sexual hunger and ignoring the obvious consequences. A week before Daryl was to return home, a frightened Katrina informed him that she was carrying his seed. By then, Daryl had fallen in love with her. He spoke to her father that evening, and the following day, they were married. Katrina's father hated Daryl for destroying his only daughter's hopes of graduating high school and attending college, but he also knew his daughter was headstrong like her late mother and would leave with Daryl with or without his permission. The following weekend, Daryl took his young bride to Brooklyn where they stayed with Ramona. Eight months later, they welcomed their babygirl Angel into the world.

Daryl's joy soured three months after his baby's birth, when he was arrested and later sentenced. Katrina stayed by his side throughout his trial, but once he was sent upstate, she took their child and moved back home with her father. Daryl received the divorce papers one year into his incarceration. Heartbroken, he held on to the legal documents for another month before giving in and granting her request.

The morning of the book fair, Angelina went to see Daryl to spend time with him before her long drive to Jenny's house in Yonkers. Angelina and Jenny were first cousins who grew up together at Taft. Jenny lived with their maternal grandmother when Ana's younger sister abandoned her at birth. Close in age, the two women developed a strong sisterly bond that maintained into their adult lives.

Daryl answered the door wearing his dark blue boxer shorts. "Hi, baby, come on in," he greeted with a smile.

As she followed him to his bedroom, she couldn't help but admire how good he looked from behind.

"How's the manuscript going?" Angelina asked, taking a seat on the edge of his bed.

Daryl rested his head on her lap and positioned his laptop on his ripped stomach. "It's going well. I got a lot done this morning. You're still heading to Yonkers?" he asked.

"Yes. I spoke to Jenny this morning. She's eager to have me all to herself. We haven't seen each other in months and have a lot of catching up to do," Angelina replied as she stroked the top of his head.

Daryl placed his laptop on the bed, wrapped his arm around her neck, and pulled her down close to him.

"I'm gonna miss you, boo," he whispered, then kissed her neck.

Angelina gently caressed his shoulders. "I know, baby. I'll be back tomorrow."

A sweet, loving woman who had given him unconditional love, there were moments when Daryl thought Angelina was the best thing that walked into his life. Yet, there were often times when her sweet demeanor scared him to the point where the urge to push her away almost overpowered his growing love for her.

Daryl quickly rose from the bed and sat on the executive chair by his desk. "Well, with you in Yonkers and Mom at my sister's house for the weekend, I'll get a lot of work done."

"Oh, that's right. Ramona did tell me that she would be at Patrice's house this weekend," she replied, rising from the bed.

Daryl's eyes gleamed as he admired the bright blue sundress hugging her luscious curves and ample bosom. His manhood stiffened and throbbed at the thought of tearing her up.

"Yeah, Patrice and her husband have been nagging Mom to visit ever since they bought their house in Maryland," he replied dryly.

Having had his mother to himself for so many years, Daryl wasn't too happy about sharing her with his long-lost sister.

Sensing his discontent, Angelina walked up behind him and started massaging his shoulders. "Baby, I know it's hard now that Patrice is back in your mom's life, but she is your sister."

"Yeah, a sister I don't even know. She probably thinks she's better than me," he replied.

"I doubt that, baby. You know she has invited us to her home numerous times. You just have to give her a chance," Angelina told him as she continued to massage his shoulders.

She took his silence as a sign that it was time for her to leave.

"Well, make sure you eat something. I know you. Once you start writing, you forget about eating," Angelina said with a smile.

"I have some leftovers in the fridge. I'll be okay."

Daryl walked with her to the front door. Angelina threw her arms around his neck and kissed him passionately before leaving.

"I'll be back tomorrow evening. I'll text you when I get to Jennie's house."

"Okay, baby. Drive safely," Daryl replied as he gently squeezed her buttocks.

Once alone, Daryl returned to his writing until the sound of his cell phone jolted him out of his comfort zone. He checked his caller ID and saw it was Budda, his upstairs neighbor and friend.

Budda was a small-time drug dealer who had lived at Foster Projects all his life. When his mother retired from the Local Teacher's Union, she moved to Atlanta, Georgia. Not ready to leave the fast paced life New York had to offer, Budda decided to stay behind. He got by on government assistance as well as selling weed to the local residents, earning enough to pay his rent and enjoy some extra perks like a dark blue Lexus LS with 21" chrome wheels, power moonroof, and a stereo system so powerful it sounded like a club whenever he drove down the street. The car's registration was in his mother's name, of course, since he didn't want his welfare benefits to get cut.

Budda wasn't much to look at, but his dealer status made

it easy for him to get sexual attention from the local chickenheads. He looked like a 350-pound, broke-ass version of rapper "T-Pain" with unkempt dreadlocks that dropped past his waistline, a gold grill that covered his front teeth, and a nappy beard that covered the huge zits he refused to treat. Angelina didn't care much for Budda. He was too flashy for her taste, and she worried he'd lure Daryl into dealing drugs again. She did her best to keep Daryl away from him without acting like a nagging girlfriend.

"Hey, playboy, what's good?"

"I'm chillin'. What you doing today?" Budda asked.

"I'm working on my second book. You know the sequel to *Betrayal* is in high demand," Daryl stated in a cocky tone.

"Shit, you gonna stay home on a nice day like today? The sun is out, and it's supposed to go up to ninety degrees, playa. You know the honeys are gonna be out there showing off that fine meat in their short shorts and tube tops," Budda replied.

Daryl let out a hearty laugh. "Man, I gotta get this book out."

"Oh, I get it. Warden Angelina's on her way to your crib, so you can't come out and play. Damn, you're pussy whooped, my man," Budda said sarcastically.

Daryl grew angry at Budda's comment.

"I ain't whooped. Anyway, Angelina is headed to her cousin's house as we speak."

"Oh shit, that's perfect! You can hang out with the boys instead of staying home in between her legs. I'm telling you, ever since you been with that woman, things aren't the same with us. I'm starting to think she did that mumbo jumbo black magic that Spanish women like doing on us brothas," Budda chimed.

Daryl laughed. "To tell you the truth, I'm starting to wonder."

"So, cut the cord and be ready by one o'clock. We can head over to the book fair and check out some fine female flesh."

Daryl thought for a minute before responding.

"You know what, I need some me time. I'll meet you downstairs at one o'clock."

"That's what I'm talking about! Later," Budda said.

When he hung up the phone, Budda leaned back on his plush Italian leather sofa and inhaled the sweet haze from his blunt. He thought about Angelina and how fine she looked every time he saw her come through with Daryl.

"That fine Latina is too much woman for that bitch-ass Daryl," he said to himself, while taking another hit from the blunt. "He thinks 'cause he's got money, a little bit of fame, and a fine woman that he's better than us. That cocksucker doesn't remember where he came from."

The ringing of his phone interrupted Budda's thoughts. Recognizing the number, his mind went into overdrive; he suddenly came up with a plan to knock Daryl down a few notches.

"You called right on time," he answered with a wicked smile.

*****

Throwing on his white wifebeater tee, jeans, and white Nike Air Force One's, Daryl made it out the door by 12:45 p.m. Before leaving, he saw his white baseball cap on the dining room table and decided it would be the perfect finishing touch to his outfit. The cap was a Father's Day gift from Angelina, and she had it personalized with the title of his book stitched in black thread across the front and in the same font as on the cover.

Daryl was waiting at the entrance of his building when Budda's car pulled into the parking lot. Daryl smiled as he walked towards him, bopping his head to the sounds of Jay Z blaring from the car speakers. As he glanced inside the car's open window, Daryl grimaced at the sight of Butta Face sitting in the passenger seat. He hadn't seen her since their last booty call. At first, she kept blowing up his cell phone leaving nasty messages, but after a few weeks, she abruptly stopped the harassment.

Daryl leaned forward, resting his forearm on the driver side window. "What up, playboy? I thought you wanted to hang out?" he asked, ignoring Butta Face.

"Hell yeah. I just thought the four of us could drive around for a while before heading to the book fair," Budda replied with a smirk.

Daryl raised his eyebrows. "The four of us?"

He then glanced towards the back seat and noticed another female sitting there. She was a young redbone with short, light brown hair and full lips that glistened whenever the sun's rays hit her cherry red lipstick. Daryl couldn't believe Budda's shit!

"Yo, get out the car for a second. I need to speak to you," Daryl said, clearly angry.

Once out of earshot, Daryl let Budda have it.

"What the fuck, man! You know everyone knows Angelina in this neighborhood. Hell, she's lived here all her life. The last thing I need is for some gossiping bitch ass telling her that I got in a car with some chick! I don't need the fucking drama."

"Playa, I understand, but I'm in a bind. I was on my way to the block when Butta Face called saying she wanted to hang out. I figured we'd take her to my crib and have some fun before heading to the book fair. But, when I showed up, she had her cousin with her. So, I thought I'd bring the cousin along. You don't have to do nothin' with her. Just keep her company while I'm doing my thing with Butta Face," Budda explained.

Then he leaned in closer to Daryl and continued in a hushed tone. "Listen, dawg, word on the street is that ever since you've been with Angelina you've gotten soft. And no disrespect to you or your girl, but I've also heard people comment on how she's much older than you. Not that she looks it, but like you said, Angelina is from around here. So, of course, everyone knows how old she is, playa."

Daryl let his friend's advice sink in.

"Maybe you're right. I'm young, handsome, and the author of one of the hottest books in the NYC. I gotta start taking care of my image, and I think being seen with a young shortie will be a good thing," Daryl responded smugly.

Budda laughed as he playfully slapped his friend's back.

"Now you talking, playa! Look, I'll drive to 112th Street and Lenox Avenue. You meet me there. That way, you don't have to chance no one who lives around here running back and telling your girl."

"Sounds good," Daryl replied.

When Daryl reached 112th Street, he quickly hopped into Budda's car. The more they drove, the more relaxed he felt; enough to enjoy the music and take a good look at the 5'5", rock solid body with dark brown bedroom eyes sitting next to him. He liked how the fabric of her pink shorts and matching tank top hugged her voluptuous curves, showing off her perky D-cup breasts. She looked like those video vixens he loved to watch on the music channels. The rise in the crotch of Daryl's pants sealed his approval.

Cruising over the Madison Avenue Bridge, they quickly merged onto the Major Deegan Expressway and arrived at the Yankee Stadium exit in no time. Budda found an out-of-the way spot by the handball courts that faced the highway. Although everyone seemed to be having a good time, Butta Face did not look happy about the situation. She didn't appreciate how Budda tricked her into bringing her cousin along for the ride. When they spoke earlier, he asked her to bring DeeDee to hang out with "his boy", only to discover that person was Daryl. She resented Daryl for dropping her soon after meeting Angelina. Now here he was sitting behind her kicking it with her cousin. How she hated the two women who occupied her paramour's time.

Budda convinced Butta Face to take a walk with him

behind the handball courts. Daryl and the young lady decided to sit by the benches facing the highway and river.

"So what's your name?" Daryl finally asked.

"My name is DeeDee. And you are Daryl, the one who wrote *Betrayal,* right?"

Daryl's chest and head swelled with cockiness. "That's right. The best damn book on the planet!"

DeeDee blushed at his statement. "I've read your book. Butta finally lent it to me, I thought it was great," she told him.

"Thank you. I'm in the process of writing part two," Daryl said while sliding closer to her on the bench.

"That's what's up. I can't wait to read it," she said, genuinely excited.

"Well, if you play your cards right, I'll let you read it before it comes out," he replied with a slight smirk.

DeeDee's face lit up. "I'd like that." She then rested her hand on his thigh. "So where's your girl today?" she inquired, trying to sound innocent.

"How do you know I got a girl?" Daryl asked, surprised.

"My cousin mentioned it. She said you were running around with some Spanish chick from the projects across from you."

"Well, yes, I have a girl. But, she's not here now, is she? I'm here talking with you," he said, putting his arm around her shoulders.

"My cousin tells me everything, like how good you are in bed. It's a shame you're faithful to your girl. I would've loved to taste your lollipop," DeeDee cooed, then raised his middle finger up to her mouth and began sucking on it seductively.

Daryl couldn't believe it. This girl was throwing herself at him, and honestly, he loved the attention.

"I'll tell you what; Budda's taking Butta Face to his crib for some fun. Why don't you and I head to my crib so we can get to know each other, and maybe…just maybe, I'll let you taste more than my finger," he told her in a seductive tone.

DeeDee gently slid her hand inside his jeans and began stroking his rock-hard tool. "I would love that."

She unzipped his jeans and let her mouth swallow his dark horse. Daryl was in heaven. She drove him wild with every stroke from her eager mouth. He wanted to shoot his hot lava down her throat, but they were interrupted by a couple of joggers approaching on the bike path behind the benches. Daryl quickly zipped up his jeans and grabbed DeeDee by the arm.

"Budda! Let's get the hell outta here!" he yelled as they walked towards Budda's car.

*****

After arriving at Foster Projects, the guys took their sexual conquests to Daryl's apartment. Wanting to spend some alone time with Butta Face, Budda quickly whisked her off to his place. That's when Daryl took DeeDee into his bedroom where she made herself comfortable by kicking off her sandals before lying across the bed on her stomach.

"You want something to drink?" he offered.

"Some liquor would be nice," she replied seductively.

"I got some Ciroc. How do you want it?"

"Straight up," she boldly replied.

Daryl went to the kitchen to get two glasses. He liked how she drank her Ciroc straight up, like she was straight hood. Angelina didn't like drinking hard liquor; she preferred chardonnay wine. When he returned to his bedroom, he almost dropped the two glasses at the sight of DeeDee. She had removed her clothes and positioned herself on his bed with her knees slightly bent and legs spread wide open as she massaged her swollen clit.

"Damn, girl! You don't waste time!" he said.

"Why don't you pour us a drink and get comfortable," she softly suggested.

Daryl quickly poured the drinks, placed them on his desk, and proceeded to remove his clothing. He joined her on the bed, and while holding the drink in one hand, he used his free hand to play with DeeDee's eager muff. Her kitty juices were flowing, and Daryl found his fingers soaked with her bodily fluids. DeeDee took a sip of his drink and let her head fall back. Her hips moved to the motion of his finger as she rubbed her swollen breasts. Arching her back, she softly pinched her nipples and moaned. Daryl loved watching her bite her lower lip and emit sounds of pleasure. Sticking two fingers inside her, he began stroking the insides of her vaginal walls while his thumb played with her clit.

Wanting to satisfy his throbbing tool, Daryl quickly mounted her, digging into her canal with fury as he threw her legs over his shoulders. Growing tired of the missionary position, he flipped her over on all fours. DeeDee moaned loudly as he dug deep inside her until he felt the need to explode. Within a few seconds, he released his load onto her smooth back and ass.

Exhausted, Daryl slowly got up and headed towards the bathroom, instructing DeeDee to stay on her stomach until he returned with a washcloth. He looked at his reflection in the mirror as he entered the bathroom. Face drenched in sweat, he felt a slight pain of guilt in the pit of his stomach as he thought of Angelina. She trusted him completely; yet, there he was doing the very thing he'd promised not to do…cheat on her. Daryl thought about it for a second longer and then shrugged his shoulders.

"What Angelina don't know won't hurt her," he told himself.

When he returned to his bedroom, any remaining feelings of guilt completely disappeared once he laid eyes on DeeDee lying on his bed looking enticing.

The two got dressed and stepped outside to get some air. He spotted Budda sitting on a nearby park bench and smoking a blunt while Butta Face talked on her cell phone.

"All good, playa?" Budda asked as the smoke from his blunt slowly escaped his lips.

"Of course. Listen, I'm gonna head back home and finish doing some more writing. You good?" Daryl questioned.

"Yeah, I'm good," Budda replied with a mischievous smile. "I'm gonna take the girls home. I'll hit you up later, my man."

"A'ight," Daryl answered before walking over to DeeDee. "Gimme your number and I'll call you later."

"Okay, daddy," she replied, then took his phone and added her digits.

A half hour later, Daryl heard his doorbell ring. For a second, he feared it would be Angelina.

"Who is it?" he called out while approaching the door.

"It's me...Budda."

Relieved, Daryl opened the door.

"Let's go to my room and talk," Daryl said as he led Budda inside.

When Budda entered Daryl's bedroom, he sniffed around like a hound dog, "Damn! It smells like sex up in here!"

"I know. I'm gonna have to sleep with the windows open to air out the room because Angelina's coming back tomorrow night."

He smiled as he poured himself and Budda a drink. Budda took his drink and leaned against Daryl's desk.

"So how was DeeDee?"

"That bitch was crazy. You know she was on my bed butt-ass naked when I got back from da kitchen? She's one freaky piece of meat," Daryl commented with a laugh.

"That's what I mean. Why you gonna tie yourself down with Angelina when you can get all da pussy you want? Men do it all da time." Budda took another sip of his drink before continuing. "You just gotta tell DeeDee that Angelina is off limits. Remind her that if she wants to keep riding with you, it's in her best interest to keep her mouth shut."

"Well, DeeDee's a grown woman, and if she knows

what's good for her, she *will* keep her mouth shut. Otherwise, the bitch will get kicked to the curb. That's my bond. I ain't leaving Angelina for a chickenhead. She's got me in the lucrative position I'm in now, and I'm not gonna let her go until I get everything I want," Daryl said with an air of conceit.

"And what's that?" Budda asked.

"The world, Budda…the world on a silver platter and Angelina's gonna serve it to me," Daryl replied, then raised his glass as if cheering his statement.

They both laughed as Daryl further shared the details of his plan.

Chapter 6
Mo' Money, Mo' Problems

"Be downstairs in five minutes!" Daryl growled through the phone.

"Baby, can you give me ten minutes? I'm helping my mother pay some bills," Angelina answered, the harshness of his tone causing her to feel nervous.

"FUCK! Then be downstairs in ten minutes, and not a minute more or I'm leaving!" he replied before hanging up.

Angelina prepared the money orders rapidly. She promised to prepare them the week before, and her mother had started nagging her because of the delay.

"Ever since you've been with that man, all you do is get up, take a shower, and wait for his phone call. I swear, Angie, you're acting like a fool! When are you gonna realize he's using you?" Ana said as she watched while her daughter frantically stuffed the money orders into the envelopes.

Angelina grew tired of her mother's badgering. Every time she was ready to go out, her mother would tell her the same thing. Ana was beginning to sound like a broken record.

"Mami, I don't have time for this. I have to go out and that's that. Can't you understand that I'm happy with Daryl? Can't you understand that he makes me happy?" Angelina asked as she got up from the table and grabbed her coat.

"Happy? Have you looked at yourself lately? You're always in a bad mood. Especially when he doesn't call you for many days! You even sleep with your cell phone next to you. You don't think I hear you crying sometimes? You think I don't notice you're drinking more than usual?" Ana voiced.

Deep inside, Angelina knew her mother was right. The months that followed her trip to her cousin's house were a nightmare. Daryl had changed in such a dramatic way that at times she felt she didn't even know him.

Angelina gathered her purse and the envelopes. "Look, Mami, I love you, but I'm a big girl now. You have to stop worrying about me. I'll be fine." With that, she kissed her mother on the forehead and headed out the door.

After locking the door behind Angelina, Ana placed her hand on her chest as she turned towards the statue of her favorite saint perched in the corner of her living room.

"Please, Virgencita, watch over my daughter. I have a bad feeling about that man," she prayed as tears flowed from her weary eyes.

As Angelina made her way down the steps, her mother's words sank in. Daryl and Angelina were always arguing about one thing or another. He would blame her if anything didn't go his way. If the books didn't arrive on time from the printer, it was her fault. If the bookstores didn't send his checks on time, it was her fault. If the stars were not aligned to his liking, IT WAS HER FAULT! It got to the point where every time her cell phone rang, she would jump nervously and be left breathless by the pounding in her chest. Daryl would call her at all hours to complain about her "incompetence". Angelina often thought about leaving him, but by the time Daryl's cruel behavior surfaced, she was head over heels in love with him. Many nights she prayed Daryl would go back to being the loving man she had met and fallen in love with.

Angelina made it downstairs in record time. As soon as she dropped her mother's bills into the nearby mailbox, she heard Daryl's car stereo blaring as he came around the corner. She swiftly made her way to his vehicle and got in. While adjusting her seatbelt, she glanced over and cringed at the angry look on his face.

"Hi, baby," she managed to say.

Not saying a word in response, Daryl shifted gears and sped off. Angelina sighed as she stared out the window. Daryl finally spoke when they turned at the corner of 112th Street and Fifth Avenue.

"Let me ask you a question," he said.

By the tone of his voice, she knew whatever he was about to ask her was not going to be good.

"What's up, baby?" she asked, her stomach knotting up from nervousness.

"Why should I stay in this damn publishing business?"

Here we go again, Angelina thought to herself as she closed her eyes in despair and massaged the bridge of her nose. She was growing increasingly tired of Daryl's threats to shut down the business. Angelina also feared he would make good on his threat. She felt if he decided he didn't want to be involved in the literary industry anymore, there was a strong possibility she would never see him again. That thought made her realize *Betrayal* was the only thing keeping them together.

A wave of panic rippled through her body at the thought of losing him. She knew she had to choose her words carefully to convince him not to give up writing. So, she collected her thoughts before speaking.

"Baby, I know you're under a lot of stress, but you must understand that this is the time of year when people are focused on getting their kids clothes and supplies in preparation for the start of school. I'm sure book sales will increase again soon."

She tried to ease his mind, but her words provided very little comfort to him.

"Listen, I got bills to pay. My baby's mom is bitching for more money, and all this fuckin' running around ain't cutting it. Hell, I make money, then have to turn around and give it to

61

the city of New York because of all the parking tickets I'm getting!" he yelled, pounding his fist on the steering wheel.

"Daryl, we've been doing pretty decent with the books. Yes, we could be doing better, but lately, it's been hard getting in touch with you, and as a result, I haven't been able to get things done. You know I don't make any decisions until I clear them with you first and…"

"I've been out here on my grind!" Daryl shouted, interrupting her. "What? Do I have to wake up every morning and check in with you first? What are you, my parole officer?"

Angelina felt the all-too-familiar pounding in her chest, and her cheeks felt hotter than the sun as her hands began to tremble. She could not control the anger building up inside of her.

"Listen, I'm not your fucking parole officer, but I *am* your fucking marketing manager! You're the boss and with that comes responsibilities, something you've been slacking on for a while now. And, on a personal note, I'm your woman. So, it would be nice if I heard from you once in a while! You know, Daryl, I'm tired…tired of you and tired of this whole damn publishing business. If you're having second thoughts about your company or me, then let us both be and go on about your damn business, whatever or whoever that business is. I'm through!"

Angelina's words escalated his anger.

"Fuck this shit!" he yelled before grabbing a small remote from the cup holder and pointing it towards the CD player.

Soon, music blasted inside the Escalade. The vibrations from the bass caused the windows to shake. That's when Angelina realized his old CD player had been replaced by a new state-of-the-art stereo system complete with a pair of giant subwoofers in the trunk. Angelina motioned for him to lower the volume.

"When did you get a new system?" she inquired.

"I got it a few days ago. The old system was giving me

problems, so I got this at a huge discount. What? Did I have to clear it with *you* before I bought it?" he sneered.

Angelina's head hurt from all the arguing. She just wanted to change the subject.

"So where are we going?" she asked.

"We're going to Trevor's crib," he replied. "He and Linda invited us to dinner. Didn't I tell you?"

"No, you didn't. I haven't seen or spoken to you in five days, remember?" she answered sarcastically.

"Well, I'm telling you now," he answered in the same sarcastic tone.

They rode in silence as he drove up First Avenue towards the Bronx's Major Deegan Expressway.

Angelina was right; Daryl was slacking. He didn't possess the drive that he once had when he first started writing. He wasn't making his rounds to the bookstores or pounding the pavement trying to move his books. Unbeknownst to her, he and DeeDee had been spending every moment together making passionate love at the same motel he took Angelina on their first date. Life was one big party for them. When they weren't off somewhere having sex, they hung out at Budda's place drinking Hennessy and smoking haze. Budda and Butta Face's relationship grew, as well. All four became the best of friends.

They arrived at Trevor's house within twenty minutes. Trevor and Daryl went way back to the days when they were toddlers playing at the Marcy Project's playground. When Daryl started hustling, he recruited Trevor to be his right-hand man. The two men ran the projects with an iron fist. It was when Trevor met Linda that he decided to get a legitimate job to provide a normal life for the woman he knew would be his wife one day.

Trevor met Linda one summer on a Saturday night at a house party Daryl threw at his mother's apartment. Trevor was eighteen and had more money than he could spend; he was living the life most people in the hood only dreamed of.

When Trevor took one look at Linda, he was smitten by her Latin swagger. Seventeen years old, Linda had a banging body with a fat booty that would make any sista jealous. Her dark brown hair with soft curls cascaded down her soft shoulders. From that night, they were inseparable.

The two decided to marry on Linda's nineteenth birthday, and using the money he had saved from him and Daryl's illegal dealings, Trevor started his own towing business. Within a year, he had a fleet of tow trucks and contracts with major agencies throughout Brooklyn. Once Trevor Jr. was born two years later, Trevor purchased a single-family brick home on Gunhill Road and moved them to the Bronx.

When Linda opened the door, she greeted Angelina with a warm hug but could see the pain shrouding her once joyful looks. As Trevor and Daryl retreated to the basement, Linda took her friend into the kitchen where she was preparing dinner.

"Are you alright?" Linda asked as she chopped the vegetables.

Angelina leaned her tired body against the cabinet. Unable to speak, she placed her hands on her face and started to cry.

"Girl, you gotta tell me what's up. Qué pasa?" Linda asked, concerned.

Angelina grabbed a sheet of paper towel from off the roll overtop the sink and gently wiped the tears streaming down her cheeks.

"I don't know, Linda. Daryl's been acting like a madman lately. He hardly calls me anymore, and when he does, it's to argue. I work my ass off to keep his company together; yet, he blames me for any little thing that goes wrong. He complains about money; yet, he just purchased a new car stereo complete with speakers," Angelina wailed.

Linda put her knife down and lovingly placed her hand on Angelina's shoulder. "I didn't want to say anything, but Trevor and I have noticed a huge change in him, as well. He

64

hardly calls us anymore. We were actually surprised he accepted our dinner invitation. He's always telling Trevor he's too busy."

Linda's heart ached as she watched Angelina continue to cry. She genuinely felt her pain.

"Baby, I'm not gonna lie. You look like shit. You can't go on like this."

"Trust me, there are times when I just want all this bull to end. But, I love him, Linda. I remember how it was with us in the beginning, how he paid attention to every detail and treated me like a queen. I know he loves me. He's just been under a lot of pressure lately. Seems like everything changed when I got back from my cousin's house a while back. Maybe I shouldn't have gone anywhere that day."

Linda rolled her eyes and angrily slammed her hand on the marble countertop. "Oh, hell no! Don't blame yourself! Your trip has nothing to do with his dumb behavior. You gotta talk to him and tell him how you've been feeling, girl. If you keep it bottled up, you will explode one day."

As she consoled her friend, the sound of footsteps coming toward them from the basement startled them.

"Hurry…go to the bathroom and wash your face, mamita. I'll call you later and we'll talk some more, okay?" Linda whispered.

Angelina quickly headed towards the rear of the house only seconds before Trevor walked into the kitchen. Linda frowned when she noticed the look of disgust on his face.

"What's wrong?" she questioned.

"Daryl's acting like an ass. I need a damn drink. Where's Angelina?" he asked, looking around.

"She's in the bathroom. Baby, I think you need to have a talk with Daryl. He's been treating Angelina like crap, and I'm afraid she's gonna have a nervous breakdown if he keeps it up. Has he talked to you?"

"No. Right now, he's on the phone with some bird he's been running around with." Trevor grabbed the bottle of cognac kept in the cabinet underneath the kitchen counter.

Linda looked at him in shock. "Oh my God! Is he fucking crazy? As good as Angelina's been to him and he's playing her? Baby, either you talk to him or I will. I will not have him ruin her life nor will I have him talking to some bird on the phone while he's here with Angelina. How disrespectful!"

"Baby, I'll talk to him. Let me handle this," Trevor reassured her, then gently kissed her on the lips before heading back downstairs with the bottle of liquor in hand.

Daryl was still on his cell phone when Trevor returned. Shaking his head in disbelief, Trevor went behind the bar, poured himself a drink, and swallowed the liquor in one gulp as he unwillingly listened to Daryl having an explicit phone conversation with DeeDee on speakerphone.

"Boo, I got my boy Trevor listening to you, too," Daryl told her as he relaxed on his friend's futon.

"That's fine with me. The more the merrier," she answered with a giggle.

Trevor sat in amazement as he heard DeeDee's moans. Everything Daryl told her to do she did with no shame. Trevor had met DeeDee once before when Daryl brought her by while Linda wasn't home. He could see by the way she sat in Daryl's truck that she was nothing but a hoodrat. She had kept her eyes on Trevor while seductively licking her lips and staring at his crotch. Trevor worried that his good friend was getting in too deep with a chick he knew wasn't worth it.

Within a few minutes, they heard DeeDee squeal with delight, an indication the vibrating dildo had done its job.

"Baby, I need you bad. Dump that bitch and come see me. You know you want to," she finally told him.

"Yeah, baby, I wanna see you, too. I'll call you around eleven o'clock tonight, okay?" Daryl answered.

"Okay, baby. Later."

Daryl ended the call and leaned back with a cocky smile on his face. "The big dog is back!" he yelled as he pounded his chest like Tarzan.

"What the hell was that all about? Yo, it ain't a good look for you to be talking to that bird with Angelina right upstairs, son. What kind of shit are you pulling, dawg?" Trevor shot back.

"Well, all you had to do was tell me to cut the conversation. What, you liked what you were hearing?" Daryl replied, flashing a devious smile.

"The reason I didn't tell you to stop is because I didn't think you'd disrespect my home by letting her continue, but I see you don't give a fuck. Damn it, Daryl. You're my boy, and we've had our share of freaks back in the day. But, I'm married now and you have a good woman, too! I hope you're not willing to fuck things up for a slut like DeeDee," Trevor scolded.

"Listen, Angelina has to understand that I'm a horny bastard. I need my variety of women," Daryl whined. "Maybe I'll settle down in a few years, but right now, I wanna do me."

Trevor couldn't believe the nonsense coming out of his boy's mouth. "Okay, playa, so have you told Angelina how you feel?"

Daryl laughed. "Hell no! If I tell Angelina I just wanna do me, it defeats the purpose of my whole plan. Trevor, you've known me ever since we were in diapers, and you know I do things for one reason and one reason only. I wanna be on top of the game and stay on top of the game. Fuck who I have to step on to get there," he voiced in a cold, uncaring tone.

"Then I guess you didn't learn shit when you did your bid upstate, huh? I thought you'd come out a better man, but I see you still have the same drug dealer mentality that got you locked up in the first place. You're gonna lose everything if you keep this up," Trevor warned.

"You just soft 'cause your ass got married and you're stuck with a kid," Daryl shot back.

Trevor glared at him as he tried to control his growing anger. "I'm gonna ignore what you just said 'cause you're my boy and you ain't thinking straight right now. But, you're changing, my friend, and I don't like who you're becoming."

Their conversation was cut short by Linda calling them up for dinner.

*****

The ride back was as quiet as the dinner. Angelina was too depressed to eat much, but she wasn't so withdrawn that she didn't notice how Trevor and Daryl hardly spoke at the dinner table. Now while they were driving, Angelina was hoping Daryl would invite her back to his place. It had been a long time since she felt his touch and she longed for him. However, when he pulled up in front of her house, her hopes of that happening were dashed.

"So what are you gonna do for the rest of the evening?" she asked him.

"What do you think? I'm gonna go home and work on my book," he answered dryly.

"Oh okay, baby. I'll see you tomorrow," she replied softly before getting out of his truck.

He didn't make any move to kiss her goodnight, and she didn't want to risk the possible rejection if she had asked.

Once inside the apartment, Angelina showered and went to bed but couldn't sleep. Her mind raced with thoughts of their beginning when things were so good between them. Now she lived in a constant nightmare. She loved him, and fear of the unknown was tearing her apart. *Is he cheating? Is the stress from his writing getting to him? Is he just using me?* There were too many questions and no answers to ease her aching heart. Linda was right; she needed to talk to him and tell him how she felt. Angelina tried calling him but got his voicemail as usual. So, she sent him a text message: *We need to have a serious talk. I can't take it anymore.*

She hoped he would answer her message right away, but to her dismay, she received no reply from Daryl. Heartbroken, she walked to her mother's kitchen and poured herself a tall glass of tequila to help her sleep.

Chapter 7
Money, Power, Respect!

The sweet aroma of eggs and bacon greeted Daryl as he awoke from his slumber. Ramona was in the kitchen preparing breakfast for her baby boy. Exhausted from his evening of marathon sex with DeeDee, a home-cooked meal would do his body good.

He slowly rolled onto his side and grabbed his cell phone from off the nightstand. As he scrolled through the many messages he had received, he paused and read Angelina's text.

Damn, I should've called her last night, he thought while slowly rising from his bed. He had a gut feeling Angelina was seriously thinking about leaving him and he wasn't having that, at least not until he accomplished his goal.

He could see the look of discontent on Angelina's face as he sat across from her at Trevor's house, but he didn't care. Angelina's feelings were irrelevant to him. All he cared about was getting paid. Thanks to her, he got what he craved: money, power, and respect.

Just like back in his days of hustling, he could wave around hundred-dollar bills. The only difference now was that the cops couldn't harrass him because he was making legit money. Angelina's know-how made him good money, and he was going to bleed her dry like a vampire. However, he knew in order to keep her around he had to keep her happy. He knew he wouldn't find anyone to go hard for him and work for free like she did. Hell, he was even considering paying for her to go to law school so he could have a pro bono attorney at his disposal.

He got up from his bed and headed straight towards the bathroom. While the hot water streamed over his body, he tried to devise a plan to gain her trust again.

Think, Daryl! You have to calm her down, he thought as he lathered his aching muscles.

As soon as he stepped foot back into his room after showering, his cell phone rang. He recognized the number right away; it was Junior, a book promoter from Atlanta, Georgia.

"What up, playboy?" Daryl answered.

"Hey, Daryl! What's poppin'? I'm calling because I'm having an end-of-summer party and would love to have you come down for a book signing. Your book is on fire here. People can't get enough of it!"

The enthusiasm in Junior's voice excited Daryl.

"That's what's up! When's the party?" Daryl asked.

"Two weeks from Friday. Come down on Thursday. I'll put you up in a hotel, and bring Angelina with you. I'm dying to meet her," Junior said.

He and Angelina had conducted business a few times over the phone. Junior loved the sound of Angelina's voice, professional yet sexy. Even more, he liked the pictures of her on Daryl's website. He thought Angelina was one hot woman, too refined to be with a thug like Daryl.

"Naw, I wanna do this solo. I don't want to disappoint my female fans. It's best if they think I'm available," Daryl told him.

"Well, it's up to you. So you're coming, right?" Junior asked.

"Hell yeah, I'll be there!"

"Cool. I'll start advertising today. Well, I'll let you get back to your business. Tell Angelina I said hi."

"Later," Daryl replied before pressing the button to end the call.

For a brief moment, Daryl felt a tinge of jealousy. Every time he talked to people in the book game, especially the males, they would ask about Angelina. They would always rave about how beautiful she was and how well she carried herself. There was times when Daryl had gone as far as to have Angelina wait in the car for hours while he handled his business. He would lie to the bookstore owners, saying Angelina didn't feel well and decided to stay in the car. He didn't want any other man near his moneymaker. Daryl knew eventually she would get tired of his bullshit and run off with someone else one day, but in the meantime, he would do whatever it took to prolong that from happening.

Suddenly, thoughts of Angelina in another man's arms made him feel uneasy. He knew if he didn't call her quick she would make good on her promise to leave him. So, Daryl quickly called her, pacing back and forth as he waited for Angelina to answer her phone.

"Good morning, baby. I just saw your text," Daryl said in a soft tone.

"Hi. What's up?" she answered coldly.

"Listen, baby, I'm sorry I didn't answer your text last night, but I got caught up with my writing. I had my phone on silent so no one would bother me. I didn't see the text 'til this morning."

"Daryl, we need to talk. Things have been crazy between us, and right now, I'm questioning if we should even stay together," Angelina replied firmly, unfazed by his smooth talk.

"Why are you questioning it?" he asked.

"I feel you're not telling me everything. Look, if you wanna cool things off between us, tell me. At least I'll know where I stand and can move on with my life. I'm a grown woman who can handle whatever you have to say. But, we need to communicate," she expressed.

"Baby, it's not that. I care about you and want you in my life. It's just that running a company is harder than I thought. I'm happy I met you, babe. You have been the best thing that walked into my life."

Daryl rolled his eyes, impressed by his own lie.

Moved by his words, Angelina's voice softened. "Baby, I want to believe you, but lately, you've been acting crazy."

"I know, baby." Daryl paused for a second. "Listen, are you doing anything right now?"

"No, I'm not," she answered, then smiled in anticipation of what he would say next.

"So why don't you meet me downstairs in an hour? I want to spend the day with my boo."

Against her better judgment, Angelina's heart melted as he spoke to her. It had been a long time since he had referred to her as his boo.

"Okay, baby. See you in an hour," she answered with enthusiasm.

Once their conversation ended, Daryl couldn't contain himself. He laughed out loud as he tossed his cell phone on the bed.

"Gotcha, bitch," he murmured as he opened his closet door and began inspecting his wardrobe.

Ramona stood outside his bedroom door after eavesdropping on his conversation with Angelina. She had grown to love Angelina like a daughter, and it pained her to know her son had become a manipulator like his father. Ramona had loved her man so much that she followed him everywhere, even to the shooting galleries when he'd get dope sick. Temptation surrounding her, she took her first hit from the crack pipe at one of those galleries and was off to the races. Soon, both were living in abandoned buildings. She did unspeakable things for the next hit, things she would have never done had she not been hooked on those deadly rocks of cocaine. Now her son was using the same mind games with Angelina that his father had used on her.

"I hope he wakes up or he'll regret what he's doing," she whispered to herself as she quietly walked back to the kitchen.

*****

Daryl did everything that day to make Angelina believe he was a changed man. He wined and dined her, catering to her every desire. To her delight, Daryl was once again the loving man she had met months earlier. If this was all a dream, Angelina did not want to wake up.

Daryl further surprised her when he drove up to the front door of his building, pulled her close to him, and began gently nibbling on her earlobe.

"How about you stay with me tonight, baby? I need you," he whispered in her ear.

Her body melted into his strong embrace; she had missed his touch dearly.

"Sure. It's been so long that I almost forget what your room looks like," she joked.

"Well, come inside and I'll remind you of a lot of things," he replied softly.

That night, she gave herself completely to him without reservation, letting him take total control of her body. He pounced on her like a wild leopard, devouring every inch of her. Afterwards, they relaxed on his bed and talked until the sun's rays crept through the slits of his window blinds. Exhausted, they finally dozed off into a deep sleep in each other's arms.

*****

Angelina slowly opened her eyes to find Daryl sitting in a chair by his desk smoking a cigarette. The sight of him wearing nothing but boxer shorts ignited her desire for him.

"Good evening, sleepyhead. I thought you'd never wake

up," he said with a smile.

"What time is it?" she asked, stretching her body.

"Well, baby, it's six o'clock. Six in the evening, that is. I'm sure you're hungry. Want me to get some Chinese food?" he offered.

"Hell yeah! I'm so hungry I can eat a horse," she replied.

Daryl jumped out of his chair and threw himself into Angelina's arms that were eagerly waiting to embrace him.

"Didn't you get enough of me last night?" he asked as he playfully buried his face between her breasts.

Angelina laughed. "You're a beast, Daryl."

"I'm *your* beast, and I'm ready to tear you up again," he replied, pulling her closer to him.

"I love you, baby."

Her eyes stung from the tears she knew were about to fall. It was the first time she had spoken those words to him, even though she had felt it long before that moment.

"I love you, too, baby." He spoke the words softly into her ear. "I know I've been acting like an ass, but I promise from this day forward to stop. You are the most important woman in my life besides my mom and daughter."

"I know it now. Now, go get us some food," Angelina replied, embracing his broad shoulders.

She took great delight in watching him throw on his jeans and t-shirt before walking out the door.

Closing her eyes, she smiled as her hands caressed the pillow where Daryl's head rested only moments ago. As the sound of the air conditioner lulled her back to sleep, Angelina dreamed she was in a dark, empty room surrounded by men whose faces she did not recognize. Wearing a silk nightgown, she trembled as they taunted her with words she could not understand. Then she saw Daryl tied to a chair after one of the men turned on the lights. He begged for her to save him. She tried to run towards him, but one of the men grabbed her by the waist, holding her back as she yelled at him to let her go. Suddenly, there was a loud gunshot. When her eyes

74

focused, she saw Daryl slumped over with blood covering his face and body.

Angelina woke up in a cold sweat and screaming. She quickly sat up and looked around nervously until she realized it was only a bad dream.

*****

Once in his truck, Daryl turned on his cell phone to find he had twenty missed calls…all of them from DeeDee. Just as he was about to call her, his phone rang.

"Where the hell have you been?" DeeDee yelled. "I've been trying to call you since last night!"

"First of all, don't yell at me, bitch! You ain't got the privilege to do so. And since when do I have to tell you where I've been?" he shot back.

"You were with that bitch Angelina, weren't you? That's why your phone was off."

"Again, I don't have to tell you where or who I'm with. You ain't my woman. You're just someone I roll around with!"

His words hit DeeDee like a freight train, adding fuel to her growing anger.

"WERE YOU WITH ANGELINA?" she yelled at the top of her lungs.

"Yeah, I was with her! In fact, she's at my crib now," he retorted.

"You bastard! You think you can come fuck me and then talk to me like I'm a piece of shit? I've got a good mind to head to your house right now and tell Angelina about us," DeeDee threatened.

Daryl was about to let her have it but abruptly stopped himself from spitting any verbal venom. Realizing he had to calm her down, he took a deep breath.

"Listen, baby, I know you're pissed, but you have to be easy. Angelina started tripping and you know she's the one who holds my business down. If she's happy, she won't bother me. Then I'll have more time to spend with you."

His soft tone calmed DeeDee's rage.

"It's just that I miss you, boo. I don't want you to leave me for Angelina like you did my cousin."

"That'll never happen, boo. But you have to be patient," he told her, trying to sound calm.

"Okay, baby. I'll talk to you later," she said in a sweet voice.

"Okay, boo. Later." Daryl blew a kiss into the receiver before ending the call.

He walked towards the corner of 115th Street and Lenox Avenue where he noticed Budda standing by the chain-link fence that separated the street from the handball court. He was there with his homeboys smoking a blunt.

"What up, Budda?" Daryl said, approaching the group of men.

Budda smiled as they gave each other a pound.

"What up, playboy? What happened to you last night? Hanging out with DeeDee?"

"Naw, I was kicking it with Angelina. She was acting up, so I had to calm her ass down. I just got off the phone with DeeDee, though. I had to calm her ass down, too. These bitches are gonna drive me crazy!" Daryl chuckled.

Budda laughed so hard he almost choked on the smoke he held in his lungs.

"How the fuck were you able to calm them down?" he asked.

"I fed them both the same line. I told them they're the most important women in my life," Daryl replied with a devilish smile.

"Damn, playa, you da man!" Budda said as he did a little dance.

"I gotta do what I gotta do, my man. Well, let me head to the Chinese restaurant and get some food for Angelina. She stayed at my crib last night."

"Okay, playa, do your thang. I'll hit you up later," Budda said, patting Daryl on his chest.

"Okay, dawg. Later."

Budda's smile disappeared as Daryl walked towards Lenox Avenue. He was growing tired of his friend's good fortune. Daryl had money, a best-selling book, and Angelina. He wanted what Daryl possessed and he planned to get it at any cost!

Chapter 8
Welcome To The ATL

Thursday morning, Daryl was pumped and ready to see Atlanta, Georgia. He had devised a plan that would keep both Angelina and DeeDee happy. First, he told Angelina he had to take a trip to Florida to see his daughter, who was acting up in school. Then, he asked DeeDee to ride with him to Atlanta. By having DeeDee with him during his trip to Atlanta, he wouldn't have to worry about her jealous ass confronting Angelina while he was gone.

Come 5:00 a.m., Daryl was ready and out the door, and by 5:15 a.m., he pulled up in front of DeeDee's apartment and was pleased to see her downstairs waiting for him with her weekender bag in hand. She wore a tight yellow sundress with white-laced sandals. As he watched her get into the truck, his male anatomy rose like a loyal soldier.

Daryl took I-95 South to the Georgia border and arrived in Atlanta by early evening. He was exhausted. Since DeeDee didn't have a driver's license, Daryl had to do all the driving.

As Daryl carried the last items into the hotel room, DeeDee noticed a camcorder with tripod tucked under his arm.

"What's the camcorder for?" she inquired.

"I want to record my signing tomorrow," he answered, while gently placing the items on the queen-size bed.

"Didn't you tell Angelina you were going to Florida?

How are you gonna explain the book signing?" she asked.

"Simple. I'll tell her that I got a call from Junior while I was in Florida asking me to come do a signing. It was last minute and on my way back to New York, so I accepted. She'll understand," Daryl replied as if he had the picture-perfect plan.

"So are you gonna tape me while we're at the party?" DeeDee asked, seductively licking her full lips.

Daryl rolled his eyes. "You ask too many damn questions, girl. Come here and suck on daddy's tootsie roll. I've been horny ever since I saw you in that outfit."

DeeDee giggled and got busy unzipping his jeans.

*****

The next day, Daryl and DeeDee ventured out to take in the sights of downtown Atlanta. He surprised her with a Louis Vuitton bag that she'd been eyeing at Macy's in the shopping mall back home. She looked on proudly as Daryl pulled out a stack of hundred-dollar bills and placed them on the counter.

Later that evening after returning to the hotel to shower and dress, they headed out to Junior's party. The event took place at a well-known club named Oasis, which was located right off I-95 in downtown Atlanta. It was about a half mile from the hotel, so they had no problems finding it.

Daryl stayed true to his thug image, opting to wear jeans, a dark blue t-shirt, and crispy white Nike Uptown sneakers. Dripping in shiny jewelry, he felt like a playa as he strutted towards the entrance. DeeDee followed closely behind him, wearing a black bareback mini dress with silver along the hem and matching black and silver sandals. She wore too much makeup and looked a bit too slutty for Daryl's taste, but he didn't care. He knew there would be better-looking women drooling over him.

As they approached the entrance, Daryl smiled at the fact

that his name and title of his book had been included on the banner draped over the club's front doors. DeeDee couldn't contain her excitement.

"Daddy, look at the banner! My man is a star!"

Daryl grabbed her arm. "Shut the fuck up! These are important people, not the assholes you're use to dealing with in your hood!" he barked.

She recoiled from his grip on her. "I'm sorry, daddy. I didn't mean to embarrass you."

"Just keep quiet and smile. Let me do all the talking. Last thing I need is your ghetto ass humiliating me."

"Oh, and I guess your precious Angelina would represent you better?" she shot back.

"As a matter of fact, she would do a hundred times better than you. She's a smart cookie. And if you're gonna start hatin' on Angelina, I can put your ass in a taxi and send you back to the hotel."

"No, daddy, don't do that. I'll behave. I promise," she pleaded.

A few feet away, Junior stood by the door smoking a cigarette and talking to a couple Hispanic chicks. Their voluptuous bodies immediately caught Daryl's eye. When DeeDee realized he was checking them out, she quickly wrapped her arm around his.

"Hey, you made it! Welcome to the ATL, playboy!" Junior exclaimed loudly as he approached Daryl and DeeDee.

Junior was in his forties but dressed as though he was still a teenager. The baggy outfit he wore hung over his skinny body like they were hanging from a clothesline in someone's backyard. His attempt at trying to be hip was overshadowed by his Jeri Curl Afro and gold front teeth, which made it look like he was stuck in the '80s.

"Thanks for having me. So what's good?" Daryl asked.

"All's good," Junior replied. "You ready to sign some books?"

"Yes, sir!" Daryl then turned towards DeeDee, who had a

81

not-so-friendly expression on her face. "Oh, by the way, this is DeeDee," he said, introducing her.

Junior extended his hand. "Pleased to meet you."

"Thank you," she said, lightly shaking his hand.

Ignoring her attitude, Junior turned his attention towards Daryl. "I need to talk to you for a second. You know how it is. Always some business to handle. Please excuse us, DeeDee."

Junior placed his arm over Daryl's shoulder and led him towards the parking lot. DeeDee tried hard to listen to their conversation as they were walking away, but the Spanish chicks giggling at her tacky outfit made it impossible.

Once they were a good distance away from the ladies, Junior spoke freely. "I thought you were coming solo?"

"It's a long story, my man," Daryl replied with a sigh.

"You should've told me that you were bringing someone. When you told me that you weren't bringing Angelina, I went ahead and hooked you up with the Puerto Rican chick in the red dress," Junior said, pointing discreetly toward the door.

Daryl glanced in her direction and cursed under his breath at the woman who had a beauty beyond compare. She stood about 5'8", had a slim build, and breasts as full as Angelina's. She wore a wrap-around Donna Karan dress that hugged her thick hips perfectly. Although lighter in skin color, the hot Latina possessed similar facial features to Angelina's. Her full lips were covered in the perfect shade of red lipstick, and her black hair flowed smoothly down to her waist.

Daryl's next question caught Junior by surprise.

"Is Miss Beauty a freak?"

"What do you mean?" Junior asked, confused by the question.

"Is she bi?" Daryl asked.

Understanding where the conversation was going, Junior smiled.

"Damn, my brotha, you're really looking to have fun this weekend, huh? Yeah, she goes both ways."

"Good. Tell the Latina hotness to chill and introduce her to DeeDee. I want them to become *good* friends," he said, licking his lips.

By midnight, the club was packed. Different media outlets provided coverage of the party attended by local supporters and those well known in the urban publishing industry. The venue was huge, with sprawling bars on each side stocked with a wide variety of wines and liquors. The dance floor was crowded as the DJ spun the latest sounds. Everyone was having a great time.

Daryl's table by the main bar had been draped in fine satin cloths, and rose petals surrounded copies of his books that were on display. The huge banner hanging overhead bore Daryl's name, and posters of his book cover were on easels positioned near the table on each side.

Daryl kept busy signing books and talking to new readers of his work. As the evening progressed, he noticed DeeDee had become very friendly with his newest conquest. They sat by the bar drinking Nuvo until DeeDee felt comfortable enough to join her new friend on the dance floor. Daryl grew aroused while looking on as they swayed their hips in unison to the beat of music. At one point, Ms. Latina slid her hand onto her dance partner's backside, squeezing her bottom. DeeDee seemed to take much delight in that.

A couple hours passed, and the party started to slowly wind down. By 3:00 a.m., the only ones left in the club were Junior and his date, Daryl, DeeDee, and Ms. Latina. When Daryl saw DeeDee head towards the ladies restroom, he jumped at the opportunity to approach the mystery woman dressed in red.

"So how did you like the party?" Daryl asked.

"I had a great time. And your girlfriend's nice," she answered, licking her lips in an enticing manner.

"First, let's get something clear. She's not my girlfriend. She's just someone I brought along for the ride. So what's your name?" he asked.

"Cristina. And you're the famous Daryl James, I see," she replied in a cool demeanor.

"Yes, I am. May I ask what a pretty girl like you is doing here by yourself?"

"Well, the plan was for me to be with you tonight, but obviously, things have changed," she answered, then reached to grab her purse from the bar.

"The plans don't have to change. Why don't you meet us at the hotel? We could get to know each other."

She thought about it for a few seconds and then smiled.

"What's your room number?"

"Room 213. Junior will tell you which hotel."

Cristina stepped close to him and gently caressed his shoulder with her hand, purposely letting her breasts brush against his arm.

"I already know which hotel. Why don't you go ahead and get yourselves ready. I'll be there in twenty minutes," she whispered in his ear.

"Oh, we'll be ready, sexy mama," he replied. Her sensual aura made him wish the three of them could teleport to the room so no time had to be wasted.

The moment DeeDee emerged from the restroom, Daryl quickly whisked her outside and towards his truck. He could tell DeeDee was feeling a bit buzzed by the way she removed her sandals and staggered barefoot across the parking lot.

During their drive back to the hotel, Daryl struck up a conversation.

"So what did you think of Cristina?"

"She was a'ight. I'm glad she kept me company," DeeDee answered, trying to hide the fact that she was attracted to Cristina.

"So you felt comfortable with her?" he asked.

"Yes. Why are you asking?" she replied, becoming suspicious with his questioning.

"'Cause I invited her back to the room so we can continue with an afterparty," he told her, then glanced down at his

84

watch. "She should be there in about fifteen minutes."

Pouting, DeeDee responded, "But I thought we were gonna party alone. I didn't get a chance to be with you all night 'cause you were so damn busy."

"Listen, you know I came down here to work. So, don't start your shit. Anyway, I saw how you and Cristina were dancing with each other. Don't tell me you wouldn't want to try her. You know it's one of my fantasies," he said, trying to coerce her.

"I know we talked about it, but I didn't think we'd be doing it tonight. This is the first time you and I have gone away together and I wanted it to be special," she whined.

"Well, this will be special for both of us. It's our first threesome," he said with a broad smile.

DeeDee gave in. "Okay, daddy. If that's what you want, then I'm okay with it. At least we'll be together."

"You know you my freak, baby," he said.

"Always, daddy," she replied, biting her lower lip.

*****

As soon as Daryl stepped inside the hotel room, he headed straight for the shower. After getting fresh, he threw on his black satin boxers and poured himself a drink as DeeDee made her way to the bathroom. The evening had been a success. The money earned that night would go directly in his pocket, and even better, he was about to get it on with two women. Daryl was in heaven for real!

He continued sipping on his drink while relaxing on the bed. Daryl had almost dozed off, when he heard a soft knock at the door. Suddenly alert, he answered to find Cristina standing there looking alluring.

"Hello, Mr. James," she said, checking out his muscular body from head to toe.

"Hello, sexy," he greeted. "Come on in."

Cristina strutted past him and sat on the edge of the bed.

"Why don't you serve me a drink?"

"Sure, baby. Is on the rocks okay?" Daryl asked, making his way to the minibar.

"On the rocks is perfect," she responded, then glanced around the room. "Where's DeeDee?"

"She's taking a shower," he replied.

Within minutes, DeeDee emerged wearing nothing but a towel wrapped tightly around her body.

"Hi, Cristina," DeeDee said, smiling as she took a seat beside her on the bed.

"Hi, lovely. You look so hot with that towel wrapped around you," Cristina cooed.

"Why don't you take off that dress and stay a while?" Daryl said while approaching them, drinks in hand.

Cristina smiled as she took a sip of her drink. Then without saying a word, she got up, stood over DeeDee, and in a seductive dance routine, she unwrapped her dress, letting it drop to the floor. Underneath, she had on a black strapless corset with satin ribbons that crisscrossed under her breasts and across her back. The thin strap of her thong disappeared into her ample bottom.

"Do you like this, DeeDee?" Cristina purred as she softly caressed her hips.

DeeDee gazed up at her in amazement. "I like it a lot."

Daryl couldn't move. The sight of Cristina towering over DeeDee had him so excited that he thought he would erupt before they even got started.

Cristina turned slightly towards Daryl and asked, "Are you gonna join us, papi?"

"Oh yes, but I wanna see you two go at it first. Is it okay if I record it, though? I promise it won't end up on the Internet."

"I don't mind if DeeDee doesn't mind." She turned to DeeDee. "Do you mind, sweetheart?"

DeeDee was so hypnotized by Cristina's beauty that all she could do was nod her head in response.

"Y'all go ahead and get comfortable while I set up the camcorder." Daryl said as he quickly gathered his equipment.

Once the camcorder started recording, Cristina removed her lingerie with the skill of a stripper, swaying her hips as she slowly undid the hooks holding her corset in place. DeeDee looked on in awe as the garment fell to the floor and she found herself facing what were the most beautiful breasts she'd ever seen. Cristina's ample assets were smooth as silk; she had the most succulent dollar-sized nipples, which DeeDee longed to taste. Without further delay, DeeDee began slowly sucking on her nipple, igniting Cristina's desire.

Cristina's tongue explored every inch of DeeDee. Positioning his camcorder close to Cristina's face, Daryl expertly captured her full lips that glistened with DeeDee's juices. He then captured the look of delight on DeeDee's face as Cristina lapped away at her kitty. DeeDee's hips moved faster as uncontrollable spasms rushed through her body, causing her to reach the highest sexual climax she had ever experienced.

Unable to contain his desire any longer, Daryl positioned his camcorder on the tripod and eagerly joined his two lovelies while the filming continued.

*****

The next morning, Daryl awoke to find DeeDee fast asleep and Cristina gone. Groggy, he retrieved his cell phone from the nightstand to check the time and noticed the missed calls from his mother's house. Fearing the worst, he dialed while getting up to stretch his body.

"Hello," Ramona answered on the first ring.

"Mommy, it's me. What's up?" he asked.

"Where are you?" she asked, sounding agitated.

"I'm in Florida," he replied.

"Don't lie to me. I just got off the phone with Katrina. She told me if you were in Florida, you weren't at her house.

So, I'm gonna ask you again. Where are you?" Ramona repeated.

Daryl's heart raced. He didn't like lying to his mother.

"Okay, Mommy, I'm in Atlanta, but keep it to yourself. Angelina doesn't know," he said in a desperate attempt to calm her down.

"Well, if you lied to me, I know you certainly lied to her, as well. Damn it, Daryl. What are you up to?" Ramona questioned.

Daryl was so deep in the conversation with his mother that he didn't notice DeeDee standing behind him. Enraged by the thought that he was talking to Angelina, she grabbed the phone from him.

"Who the fuck is this?" DeeDee yelled into the receiver.

"This is Daryl's mother! Who the hell are you? And how dare you talk to me like that!" Ramona shot back.

Shocked into silence, DeeDee quickly gave the phone to Daryl and ran to the bathroom. She knew her actions would cost her dearly.

"Now I see why you didn't want me to know. Daryl, is that DeeDee? I told you to stop messing with that slut. She's gonna cause problems between you and Angelina. *Leave that girl alone*," Ramona pleaded.

"I'm a grown man! Anyway, I'm tired of being tied down to one woman. I need my freedom," Daryl retorted.

"And you think being with DeeDee gives you the freedom to do what you want? From what I hear, she's nothing but a two-bit slut along with her cousin Sandra. You've changed a lot, Daryl, and not in a good way. You're going to lose it all," she begged.

"Look, Mommy, I don't want to argue with you. You will just have to trust me when I say I know what I'm doing. Okay?"

"I will not be a part of your lies. If you want to keep doing what you're doing, it's up to you. But, remember, what you do on this earth you pay for on this earth," she said before hanging up.

"DeeDee, get your ass out here!" Daryl yelled.

DeeDee emerged from the bathroom wearing a pair of Hello Kitty pajamas. The look of fear on her face matched the tremble of her limbs.

"I'm sorry, baby. I thought it was Angelina."

"Who the fuck do you think you are grabbing my phone like that! And what if it was Angelina? Don't you realize your stupid act could have cost me everything, bitch?" he growled.

"Look, I'm tired of you putting Angelina before me when you know I make you feel better than her. I've done everything possible to prove my love to you, including our little threesome last night! All you're concerned about is Angelina and your precious company! Well, I don't feel bad for what I did. In fact, I feel so good about it that I have a good mind to march over to Angelina's house when we get back and tell her everything," she yelled in defiance.

Unfazed by her threat, Daryl smiled. "You ain't gonna do shit. And don't flatter yourself. You will never be more of a woman than Angelina; she has class. You know what? My mother was right. You're nothing but a slut just like your cousin."

Daryl's words cut deep into DeeDee's heart, shattering it into a million pieces.

"No, I'm more of a woman because I'm carrying your child. That's right, Daryl, I'm pregnant," she disclosed as tears flowed down her cheeks.

Daryl's body froze at her statement. "You're fuckin' joking, bitch!"

She walked over to Daryl. "I'm not joking. I wanted to surprise you with the news over the weekend. Now you have to leave Angelina and be with me. I'm having your baby, Daryl, and there's nothing you can do about it."

Daryl saw his whole world crumble before his eyes. With DeeDee pregnant, he'd lose Angelina as well as his dreams.

Unable to control his rage, Daryl slapped her so hard that her slender body flew across the bed and landed on the floor. DeeDee screamed as she crawled towards the corner of the hotel room. Fearing for her life, she continued to scream while caressing her bruised cheek.

Daryl stormed towards her and grabbed her by the neck as her trembling body gasped for air.

"You ruined everything, bitch! You knew I didn't want any more babies; yet, you let yourself get pregnant? When we get back to New York, you're gonna get an abortion and then get the hell out of my life. And I swear if you ever come near Angelina or me, I'll kill you. You hear?"

Fearing the worst, she agreed.

"Now get your ass up and get ready. We're going back to New York today," he said before storming towards the bathroom.

Paralyzed with fear, she stayed in place until she heard the sound of running water. DeeDee then rose slowly from the floor and walked over to the mirror to examine the bruises on her neck and right cheek. As she stared at her reflection, her fear quickly turned to anger.

"You're not going to get away with this, Angelina. You will pay, bitch," DeeDee whispered as tears flowed from her eyes.

Chapter 9
The Moment of Truth

Angelina relished in the peace and quiet surrounding the apartment she shared with her mother. Feeling guilty about her mother's loneliness as she took care of Daryl's business, Angelina had urged Ana to spend the week with her cousin Jennie in Yonkers.

"Why don't you come with me?" Ana asked her while packing.

"No, Mami. I want you to go to Jennie's house and have fun. Besides, I have a lot of things to do here while you're gone. I want to spend the week submitting my resume so I can get back to work. I miss working a nine-to-five," Angelina said with a smile.

"Oh, I think that will be good for you, mamita. I know you love working," Ana replied enthusiastically.

Angelina had wanted to go back to work for quite some time but had been so consumed with helping Daryl become a successful author that she put her idea on the back burner. However, she was more determined now than ever because she wanted to get her own apartment. She knew with her great credit it wouldn't be a problem finding an apartment, but most landlords would ask for paystubs and W2's. She wanted to be prepared when she found the right place for her and Daryl to share. Although she hadn't asked him yet, she knew once he saw the place, he would pack up and move in with her.

Since Daryl's return, Angelina noticed a change in him again. Although they didn't argue, he hardly spoke and was always in deep thought. She tried talking to him, but he would always avoid her by saying he had some personal business to take care of. She figured with her mother gone, it would be a great time to invite Daryl over for dinner and hopefully convince him to spend the night. She was looking forward to sharing her plan for their future together with him that evening.

Angelina went to the grocery store to buy the items needed to prepare Daryl's favorite meal: t-bone steaks smothered with onions and mashed potatoes. Once home, she prepped the food while the sounds of smooth jazz played on the radio. She smiled at the thought of fully pampering him.

While the steaks were marinating, she took that time to relax on the sofa and sift through the mail. She immediately noticed a yellow manila envelope addressed to her, but it had no return address. Checking its contents, she pulled out a handwritten note along with a DVD.

Hi, Angelina. I'm sending this DVD just for you! When you're done viewing it, give me a call at 646-555-6421.

DeeDee

Angelina's mind raced as she read the note several times. *Who is this?* she thought to herself. After convincing herself it was some author seeking a publisher, she turned on her television and inserted the DVD into her player.

Nothing could have prepared her for what she was about to view. There on the screen was the love of her life having a threesome with two women she had never seen before. Tears fell from her eyes and down her cheeks as she watched the images of Daryl's tryst. Angelina then noticed the date of the recording in the bottom left-hand corner of the screen, turning her pain to anger. It was the same date he told her that he would be in Florida!

As instructed, she nervously dialed the telephone number written on the note. A young woman answered on the third ring.

"Is this DeeDee?" Angelina asked.

"Yes, it is," DeeDee answered, sounding elated that she had called.

"My name is Angelina."

"Oh yes, I've heard so much about you," DeeDee replied.

The sarcasm in her tone angered Angelina.

"Look, I don't know who you are, but I just got a DVD. I'm guessing it was sent by you."

"Yes, I sent it. Why don't we meet and talk?" DeeDee suggested.

"Yes, why don't we do that? There's a café on First Avenue between 115th and 116th Street called Rum. Can you be there in an hour?" Angelina asked, trying her best to stay calm.

"An hour's fine," DeeDee answered.

Angelina set her phone down and found herself unable to move. Her knees were weak and her heart raced at the thought of Daryl's betrayal. He knew Angelina loved him with all her heart. Still, he took her kindness and generosity for granted. Big mistake.

*****

Too nervous to drive, Angelina decided to take a taxi and arrived at the café fifteen minutes early so she could have a drink before meeting with the woman who ruined her life in a matter of minutes when she sent the video. Not knowing what to expect, she opted to wear jeans, a bright green turtleneck, and her favorite Gucci boots. Angelina even pulled her long locs into a neat ponytail so they wouldn't obstruct her view. She would not be caught slipping.

Needing to calm her nerves, she ordered a double shot of

tequila. After downing the shot, Angelina kept her eyes fixed on the front door until she saw a petite woman walk in. She immediately recognized her as one of the participants on the DVD. DeeDee sashayed her way towards her, and taking a seat on the barstool next to Angelina, she ordered a vodka with cranberry.

"You must be Angelina. I saw your picture on Daryl's website," she said with an annoying smirk.

"And you must be DeeDee, the slut I saw on the DVD," Angelina shot back.

"You can call me what you want. All that matters is that Daryl calls me his boo," she responded proudly.

Angelina firmly held her drink, trying to avert the temptation of smashing the glass upside DeeDee's head. Keeping her composure, Angelina continued the conversation.

"So how long has Daryl been calling you his boo?"

"Well, girl, let me tell you. He's been calling me his boo ever since we met the day of the Harlem Book Fair. You see, he told me that you were away somewhere, and he looked so lonely I just couldn't leave him alone. So, we hung out with Budda and my cousin Butta Face for a while. Then he took me to his mom's crib where I gave him the best loving he ever had. I honestly thought he was going to tear me up that night with his huge cock, but I'm a real woman who can handle anything," she voiced.

Her vulgar words intensified Angelina's anger. She couldn't believe Daryl would spend any time with someone as vile as DeeDee, but then again, there was a lot about Daryl's past she didn't know.

"Listen, you little bitch, what you don't know about me is I'm too much of a woman to fight over any man. If he wants to be with a slut like you, so be it! But, if you think I'm gonna sit here and let you talk to me like you're better than me, you are mistaken. You don't know what I'm capable of doing to your ass!" Angelina threatened.

Angelina's words took DeeDee by surprise. She expected to hurt her, make her suffer. She hadn't anticipated Angelina to fight back.

"You're fucking crazy! You're just mad because he grew tired of your old ass and is now with someone as fabulous as me," she retorted.

DeeDee's last statement brought the ghetto out of Angelina, who slammed her drink on the bar, drew back her fist, and punched DeeDee square on the bridge of her nose. DeeDee's body hit the hardwood floor like a ton of bricks falling from a construction site! As DeeDee lay there in shock, Angelina casually went in her Gucci purse and threw a hundred-dollar bill onto the bar.

"This should cover both our drinks," she told the stunned bartender, who quickly snatched up the money and went on with business as usual.

Angelina then casually retrieved her belongings and headed towards DeeDee, who was still sprawled out on the floor.

"As I said before, bitch, you can have him. I wish you luck with Daryl. You're gonna need it."

And with that, she walked out the door.

When Angelina got home, she gathered all of Daryl's belongings, including his paperwork, and threw it into a cardboard box. She tore up all the photos of them together and deleted her information off his website and social networks. She was determined to remove any reminders of Daryl from her life. Angelina then picked up the box and stormed towards his apartment.

Arriving at Daryl's doorstep, she kicked the door with all her might. A stunned Ramona answered.

"Hi, Angelina. Are you okay?" she asked nervously.

"No, Ramona. Is Daryl home?" Angelina was unable to conceal her anger.

"Yes, he's in his room," Ramona answered, surprised by Angelina's coldness towards her.

Angelina stormed past her and headed straight towards his bedroom. She didn't think twice as she kicked open the door, causing it to slam against his bed. Startled, Daryl jumped up from his bed.

"What the fuck are you doing?" he asked.

Once inside the bedroom, she slammed the box onto the floor.

"Consider this my resignation, asshole! You're nothing but a bastard who uses people! Guess where I'm coming from, Daryl? I was at Rum talking to some bitch named DeeDee. And do you know what she told me? She said you and her have been together since the Harlem Book Fair! How could you do this to me after all I've done for you?" she said, tears welling up in her eyes.

Daryl grabbed Angelina by the arm, twisting it so hard that her muscles began to ache.

"What the fuck are you talking about? I don't know no bitch named DeeDee! You need to get proof before you come disrespecting my mother's house!" he yelled.

She snatched away from him and grabbed the DVD from the box, waving it inches from his face.

"I have proof! DeeDee sent this to my house. It shows the two of you having a threesome with some other hoe! You want to talk about disrespect, Daryl? You disrespected me and my mother's house when you allowed that bitch to send this," she boldly stated, then threw the DVD at him.

At that point, Daryl realized he had indeed been caught.

"Angelina, please…I can explain."

"What can you explain, Daryl? That while I was working my ass off, you were out there running around with God knows who? I was faithful to you when I shouldn't have been! I was there for you," she yelled.

"Look, I know you're upset and all, but stop yelling in my mom's house. Anyway, you worked your ass off 'cause you wanted to. I could do what you do in a heartbeat. I'm a big dawg in the game, and I don't need you!"

96

Angelina laughed. "You think you're the only one in the game? You think before I met you that I was some isolated woman who didn't know shit? Remember, I have worked for big companies in the past and know how to conduct myself. If anything, I could get a job with another publishing company in a heartbeat!" she yelled back as she snapped her fingers.

Before Daryl had a chance to lunge at Angelina, Ramona stormed in. Standing between the two, she grabbed at Daryl's arms.

"Stop it!" she shouted.

Angelina stepped back, glaring at Daryl with pure hate. "I don't want to have anything to do with you. Not now, not ever! You hurt me and I'll never forgive you for this!"

Exhausted, Angelina walked out the door and out of his life.

"I told you messing with DeeDee would bring problems, but you didn't listen, boy," Ramona chastised as she picked up sheets of paperwork scattered all over Daryl's room.

"I don't wanna hear it! Angelina was disrespectful towards you and me. Who does she think she is storming in here like she owns me?

Ramona looked at her son in disbelief. "She was the one helping you with your book. And while Angelina stayed home working, you ran around with DeeDee! As a woman, I know the pain that poor girl is feeling."

Ignoring his mother, Daryl got dressed. He was about to take care of things once and for all.

"Where are you going?" Ramona asked. "Don't tell me you're heading over to Angelina's house?"

"No, Mom. I'm going to look for DeeDee. She caused this problem and she's gonna pay," Daryl stated, then stormed out of the apartment.

Daryl sped up Lenox Avenue to 127th Street and parked near DeeDee's building. Careful not to be seen by anyone who knew him, he parked across the street about four cars away from the front door of the building. When he saw her coming up the block, he bolted from his truck and ran towards her. Before she could react, he shoved her against the storefront gate, pinning her between the cold metal and his body. Daryl's hand gripped her cheeks.

"What the fuck did you do, DeeDee?" he growled.

"I did what I had to do! You're going to be mine, Daryl, whether you like it or not! Don't forget, I'm having your baby," she replied, trying to push him off her.

Daryl released his grip in disgust. "And you think that by pulling this little stunt you're gonna be with me? Your actions proved you can't be trusted, bitch. As for your pregnancy, you're terminating that shit. I don't want that fucking baby and I don't want you!"

"You don't mean that, Daryl," DeeDee pleaded, choking back tears. "Once the baby's born, you'll change your mind."

Daryl looked at her with the eyes of a man possessed. "If I have to drag your ass to the abortion clinic and pull that kid out of you myself, trust me I will. I'm gonna make the arrangements and you better not disappear, bitch, or I'll hunt you down and kill you myself."

Daryl wiped his t-shirt in disgust as he walked towards his truck, leaving DeeDee standing there devastated and crying uncontrollably.

Chapter 10
The Meltdown

Christmas and New Year's are the worst times of year for one's heart to be broken, and Angelina's holidays were going to be dreadful.

After that fateful day when she learned of Daryl's betrayal, Angelina fell into a deep depression filled with loneliness and booze. It started with having a few drinks before going to bed to help her sleep, and before she knew it, she was consuming two bottles of tequila daily. It got to the point where Ana became worried that her daughter had inherited the very disease that plagued her for most of her life. Alcohol-free for fifteen years, Ana didn't want her only child to follow the same destructive path she once walked.

Adding to Angelina's depression was Daryl's persistent harassment, which made her life miserable. He sent constant text messages filled with threats and accusations. Daryl spread rumors accusing her of embezzling funds from his company's bank accounts. He also claimed she fraudulently tampered with his corporate documents in an attempt to gain control of his business. In addition, he had his mother convinced that his lies were true, turning Ramona's love for Angelina into pure hate. At Ana's urging, Angelina changed her cell phone number, giving her new digits to trusted friends and relatives only.

It was early evening on New Year's Day, and Angelina

was lying on her mother's sofa trying to get through another hangover. Her head was pounding, which meant the four aspirins she had taken thirty minutes ago had not kicked in. The shrieking sound of her ringtone interrupted her silence. She checked the number on her caller ID before answering.

"Hello," she said in a hoarse voice.

"Hey, Angelina, are you okay?" Linda asked.

"Yeah, I just woke up," Angelina replied.

Linda knew better. Years of experiencing her own family's descent into alcohol and drugs taught her to quickly recognize the signs. She didn't have to see Angelina in person to know her friend was drinking herself to death.

"Angelina, I just wanted to tell you that Trevor and I miss you. We would love to have you over for dinner next weekend."

"I don't know, Linda. I wouldn't be good company," Angelina said as she sat up slowly.

"Girl, you have to get out of the house and face the world. It's New Year's Day for God's sake."

"Don't remind me, okay! The last thing I need is for anyone to remind me what day it is," Angelina snapped at her friend.

"Look, Angelina, I know you've been through a lot, but it doesn't give you the right to come out your face like that. I'm here for you, but you have to stop your shit and get yourself together," Linda shot back.

Angelina felt a painful throb bang against her temples; her head felt like she had a high school band pounding their drums inside her brain. She didn't want to argue. She just wanted another drink.

"I'm sorry. I just need to take a shower and get something to eat. Can I call you later?" she asked.

"Okay, girl. Listen, I just want you to be happy. Hang in there and be strong," Linda replied.

Angelina put down her phone and grabbed the fifth of tequila she kept close by. Not bothering to get a glass, she took a huge swig directly from the bottle. The liquor burned her throat as it made its way through her insides. Happiness seemed to be an emotion that was always shortlived in her life. Sure, God allowed her to experience some moments of happiness, only to snatch them away when she got too comfortable. *"God has jokes,"* she would always say.

By her third swig, the hangover she felt a short time earlier had left her body, replaced by the high she grew to enjoy. When she was drunk, all of the pain went away. She would turn on her radio and dance with her imaginary knight in shining armor who loved her unconditionally. He didn't hurt her; he always chose her over anyone else. She loved him, even if he only existed in her mind.

Feeling high, she staggered towards her mother's room, only to find it empty. Searching her memory banks, she remembered her mother had gone to her cousin Jennie's house the night before to ring in the New Year. Ana had asked Angelina to join them, under the condition that she wouldn't drink. Angelina wasn't having that, though.

She made her way back to the living room, where she noticed the near empty bottle of tequila on the floor. Knowing she would need another fifth to get her through the night, she decided to go to the liquor store on Lenox Avenue before it closed for the evening. Without so much as taking a shower and still dressed in her blue cotton pajamas, she threw on her coat and headed out the door.

Too drunk to walk, Angelina decided to take her car, which was parked on 115th Street between Madison and Fifth Avenue. As she eased out of the parking space, her foot accidently pressed down on the accelerator and her tires shrieked towards Fifth Avenue. The last sound she heard was a loud crash.

*****

Angelina felt cold and frightened as she sat on the folding

chair inside the holding cell of the 25th precinct on 119th Street between Lexington Avenue and Park Avenue. Her wrists ached from the handcuffs pressing tightly around them. As her mind cleared, she remembered running a red light at the intersection and a yellow cab speeding through Fifth Avenue. The impact was still a blur. Neither she nor the other drivers were hurt, but Angelina was arrested on suspicion of DWI.

The following morning, she went before the judge and was formally charged with DWI and trying to flee the scene of an accident. Her attorney informed her that according to police reports, she continued speeding west towards Lenox Avenue following the collision until a gypsy cab gave chase and trapped her at a red light. Angelina was held on $1,000 bail. With no access to her checking account, she had to wait until her mother could come up with the money to bail her out.

Angelina was sent to Riker's Island the next morning since there was no women's jail available downtown. While waiting to be fingerprinted and medically cleared, she spent the day trying to rest her weary body on the cold steel platforms that were no wider than a newborn's bassinet. By evening, she was given the standard wool blanket and toiletries for her transfer to the Rose M. Singer Center, the only section that housed female inmates.

While waiting in line for her assigned cell, Angelina looked around to familiarize herself with her new surroundings. The housing unit was made up of two stories with rows of steel doors on each end. The bright florescent lights above hurt Angelina's eyes, and the entire area from floor to ceiling was covered in grey paint. The center of the facility was as big as a basketball court and seemed to be reserved for recreation. There were plastic tables and chairs and what looked like a 1950's style television at the far end of the room.

A loud, abrasive voice coming from a female inmate

sitting at a nearby table interrupted Angelina's concentration. Fellow inmates who hung on her every word surrounded her. The light-skinned, brash inmate had dark-colored eyes and long curly hair that cascaded over her shoulders and down her back. Her facial features resembled that of an exotic flamenco dancer from Spain. Angelina didn't understand what she was talking about but knew well enough to stay out of her way. Although never arrested in her life, Angelina was well aware of what to do and not do while locked up. Anyone with common sense knew to keep to themselves, trust no one, and steer clear of inmates with brash attitudes because they were the type who would get you into trouble. Yet, as Angelina glanced towards the table, she couldn't help but get the feeling she knew the woman from somewhere. Too exhausted to give it any more thought, she went to her assigned cell and slept.

The next day, Angelina woke up to the sound of guards announcing that breakfast would be served in ten minutes. She hadn't had anything to drink in the past twenty-four hours and her stomach ached for something to fill its void. Breakfast consisted of mushy instant oatmeal and weak coffee. To Angelina, who hadn't been eating much lately, it was like having a five-star meal. She quickly devoured the contents of her tray before heading to the shower for a much-needed cleansing.

With towel and toiletries in hand, she made her way to the showers by the guard's post. There were six stalls with no shower curtains for privacy; the only curtain available was drawn across the front entrance to shield them from the recreation room.

When she walked in, the abrasive woman she had seen the prior evening was showering in one of the stalls. Angelina removed her clothes while avoiding eye contact. As she walked towards one of the unoccupied stalls, the image of her mother home alone flashed through her mind, causing her to break down into tears.

"Hey, are you okay?" the woman asked as she wrapped her towel over her breasts.

"I'm thinking of my mom. She's eighty-one years old and had a heart attack a few years back. I'm so scared of losing her because of my stupidity," Angelina replied.

"Wow, sorry to hear that. I'm pissed, too. I have a book release party for one of my newest authors and got busted on a bullshit charge. They got me on a DWI, but because I'm on parole, the bastards are keeping me in this hellhole," she said.

When she mentioned the book release party, Angelina remembered receiving an electronic invite to a book release party hosted by Desire, CEO of Paradise Publications, an established urban publishing company. Angelina had read her bio one day when she came across one of Desire's novels in Daryl's car. Desire was not only a publisher; she also wrote three novels while incarcerated and self-published them once she got home. In addition, she ran a popular bookstand on 106th Street and Third Avenue in East Harlem. When Daryl would visit her stand, Angelina always waited in the car while he stepped out to talk to Desire. Observing her through the car's tinted window, Angelina could see Desire had the inner confidence she longed for.

"What's your name?" Angelina asked, wanting to make sure she was the same person.

"My name is Eva Rodriguez, but my pen name is Desire," she replied with pride.

At that moment, Angelina felt a surge of relief run through her body.

"Desire, I'm Angelina Rivera of Mo' Money Publishing!"

Both women stared at each other for a few seconds before yelling at the top of their lungs. As if they were long-lost friends, they hugged and cried in the middle of the shower room. When they finally released each other, Desire trotted to the wooden benches and quickly began to dress.

"Girl, go shower and meet me in the recreation area ASAP! We need to talk."

104

*****

After Angelina showered and dressed, she hurried to meet with Desire. The two women sat by the kitchen area and talked privately. Desire listened in shock as Angelina poured her heart out, sharing with her the events that led to her ending up at Riker's Island.

"That fucking bastard!" Desire huffed.

"I know. He doesn't even acknowledge he had a relationship with me. He's going around telling everyone that he's too young to be tied down to anyone. You know, Desire, I worked my fingers to the bone to get his book out there. I made phone calls, delivered his books, everything. And while I was taking care of his business, he was running around with other women. If he would have told me he wanted his freedom, I would've backed off immediately, but instead, he always assured me otherwise," Angelina said, sounding somber.

Desire seemed surprised. "Why is he saying that now, when he would always tell me that you were his girlfriend?"

"I don't know, girl. But, right now, the only thing I'm concerned about is getting out of here. I messed up badly and I need to fix this."

Desire nodded her head in agreement. "The first thing you have to do is call home. Your mother must be worried about you. Go 'head, girl."

Angelina walked over to the telephones a few feet away. Within a few minutes, she was talking to Ana.

"Ay, mamita! Are you okay?" Ana cried out when she heard her daughter's voice.

"Mami, please don't cry. Yes, I'm okay, but what's going on with my bail?" Angelina asked.

Once she composed herself, Ana was able to speak clearly. "Well, mamita, the family has put our money together, but we're short four hundred dollars. We should have the rest by tomorrow. I will get you out as soon as I have the full amount, okay?"

"Okay, Mami. I just want you to know I'm sorry. I didn't mean for this to happen," Angelina expressed, choking back tears.

"I know, my child. We'll talk about this when you get home. For now, all that concerns me is you getting out of there," she replied.

"I know, Mami. I'll call you tonight, okay?"

"May God bless you and keep you safe. You'll be home tomorrow, I promise," Ana told her.

After placing the phone's receiver back on the hook, Angelina walked over to where Desire was chatting with another inmate. When she saw the look of despair on Angelina's face, Desire got up and embraced her firmly.

"You okay, mama?" Desire asked.

Angelina had no energy left. She felt her whole world crumbling into an abyss.

"I don't know what to do."

Desire led her to some empty chairs where they sat while Angelina sobbed.

"What did your mother say?" Desire asked.

Angelina took a few deep breaths before speaking.

"My mom told me that they have six hundred dollars and should be able to come up with the rest by tomorrow."

"Good. Listen, you and I don't know each other well, but I do know of your reputation. Contrary to what Daryl says, many in the industry know if it weren't for you, he wouldn't have sold as many copies of his book as he has! All I will say is he's not well liked among his peers. He's nothing but a cocky asshole trying to be all that with the big boys. Trust me when I say this," Desire told her. "Now, what I want you to do is go to your cell and splash some cold water on your face, then come back here. We need to talk business."

Angelina nodded and then headed upstairs.

They spent that afternoon talking about everything from the literary industry to men. Angelina laughed as Desire joked

106

around with the other inmates; she felt better as the day went on. Observing Desire as she chatted with the other women, Angelina realized that underneath Desire's rough exterior was a woman who had been through a lot herself. She spoke lovingly of her son, who was eight years old and staying with her mother while she was away.

"I can't wait to see my little boy," Desire said, trying to hide her pain.

Angelina put down her book and gave her a reassuring smile. "You will, Desire. Soon, we'll both be out. Then you can spend time with your son and continue running your business. I, on the other hand, have to figure out what I'm going to do with my life. Now that I'm no longer working with Daryl, I have to see about doing something else. It's a shame because I really liked working in the industry."

"And what makes you think you're going to stop working in the industry?" Desire asked.

Angelina gave her a strange look. "What are you saying?"

"What I'm saying is, I listened to you while we were talking about the industry and you're very knowledgeable. You know what you're doing. I need people like you on my team. So, if you want, you can work with me."

Angelina didn't know whether to laugh or cry. She thought her days in the book game were over, and she certainly didn't think someone as well known as Desire would give her a chance.

"Are you serious?"

Desire leaned towards her until they were eye to eye.

"Honey, if there is one thing about me, it's that I take my business seriously. When I see talent, I grab it with both hands before the next one does. And you, Ms. Angelina, have talent. You just need someone like me to bring out the diva in you."

"Well, I don't know about me having any diva inside me, but I would love to work for you, Desire."

"Oh, you have it, my love," Desire told her. "And I'm

gonna be the one to make that diva shine. So, with that, my dear, you're hired!"

Desire put Angelina to work immediately. With Desire's cell phone in the property room at Riker's, she didn't have access to any phone numbers in the industry. However, Angelina assured her that she could get a hold of anyone either through telephone or email. While working with Daryl, she acquired a lot of mutual contacts. By late evening, Angelina decided to take a break and call her mother. To her surprise, her cousin Jenny answered.

"Hey, Jenny, what's up? Where's Mami?" Angelina asked in an upbeat tone, figuring her cousin had come up with the rest of the money needed for her bail and that was the reason she was at her mother's.

"Angelina, listen and please be calm once I tell you this. Titi Ana had another heart attack and had to be rushed to the hospital. I just spoke to the doctor and he said she's still in a coma. We got your bail together, so I'm heading downtown tonight to get you out. Just hang in there…"

Those were the last words Angelina heard before collapsing on the concrete floor.

Angelina awoke in the prison infirmary. Desire stood over Angelina stroking her hair with a worried look on her face.

"Hey, girl, you woke up. It's about time," Desire said.

Remembering Jenny's words caused Angelina to experience an instant anxiety attack.

"Oh my God, Desire, I gotta get out of here! My mom's in the hospital!"

"I know. When you fainted, I spoke to your cousin. She told me everything. Look, Angelina, you need to calm down so you can get up out of this infirmary and get home to your mother."

At that moment, the doctor walked in.

"Good evening, Ms. Rivera. Welcome back," he said as his eyes scanned her chart. His wire-rimmed glasses rested on the tip of his thin nose, and the fluorescent lights in the room reflected off of his balding head.

"Hi, Doctor. So when can I leave the infirmary?" Angelina asked.

"Well, I have to run some tests, but I feel you should be back in your cell in a few hours, just in time to head home," he replied.

Surprised, Angelina sat up on the bed.

"Head home? You mean my bail's been paid?"

"According to the C.O., your bail's all set. You'll be going home, young lady," he said with a smile.

*****

By the time they finished processing her to be released, Angelina didn't get home until the next morning. She quickly showered, put on some clean clothes, and headed to the hospital. She arrived at Mount Sinai on Fifth Avenue by taxi and went directly to the ICU on the ninth floor. Once in her mother's room, she noticed Jenny sound asleep on the plush recliner next to the hospital bed where Ana lay with tubes coming out of her nostrils and mouth. Ana's face was pale and ashy, and her short gray hair stood up on end. Angelina quietly walked over to her mother, tears flowing as she held her frail hand.

"Mami, it's me…Angelina. Mami, please wake up," she pleaded.

Angelina's words caused Ana's eyes to flutter. Then she forced them to open and squeezed her hand lightly. She looked into her daughter's eyes as she mustered a faint smile around the tube lodged inside her.

"Yes, Mami, it's me. It's Angelina. I'm here to take care of you."

The monitor positioned above the hospital bed mimicked the beating of Ana's heart. Suddenly, her heart rate increased, and she squeezed her daughter's hand with all her might. They looked into each other's eyes for a few seconds before

Ana's eyelids became heavy and her grip grew limp. Just then, the monitor let off a continuous steady sound.

Chapter 11
Transformation

The day Ana Rivera de Dalmau left this earth was the most devastating day of Angelina's life. Ana's life insurance named Angelina as sole beneficiary, granting her all rights to ensure that Ana's last wishes were carried out. Ana wasn't one who liked tradition. Therefore, as per her wish, she was laid to rest in a cherry oak casket. Her body peacefully lay dressed in white satin from head to toe. Angelina chose a beautiful satin headdress that made her mother look like a 1930's movie actress.

Angelina looked equally as stunning dressed in a white Donna Karan suit with white Jimmy Choo pumps. She made sure to represent her mother with style and grace, just as Ana would have wanted. The two hundred plus mourners in attendance wore white, as well. Ana had spent her entire adult life living in El Barrio and was loved by all in her neighborhood. So, Angelina saw it fit to hold her wake at Farenga Funeral Home on 116th Street between Second and Third Avenues.

Desire was still at Riker's but kept in touch with Angelina daily through telephone calls. She assured Angelina that her position with Desire's company would be available whenever she was ready.

On the evening of Ana's wake, Angelina stood outside the funeral home. Lighting up a much-needed cigarette, she leaned against the gold railing on the steps. She hadn't touched a drop of liquor since her prison release and made a promise to herself to stay away from the sauce. The cold January breeze embraced her as her body shivered underneath the dark wool coat. Just then, she noticed a familiar black BMW parking just a few feet away from the entrance. She smiled as she saw Trevor and Linda emerge from the vehicle, but her joy turned to anger when she saw the back door open and Daryl step out of the same vehicle. Enraged, she threw her cigarette on the sidewalk and stormed towards the car. Before she could jump on Daryl, Trevor and Linda quickly grabbed her.

"What the hell are you doing here?" Angelina growled as she fought to escape their grip.

"Angelina, calm down," Trevor pleaded. "Daryl came to pay his respects."

"Respects? That son of a bitch doesn't know anything about respect! How dare you show up at my mother's wake after what you did to me? How dare you, Daryl?" Angelina shouted.

"Look, I'm here to show respect. No matter what you did to me, I had mad respect for your mom. You should be happy I still care," Daryl responded with his usual arrogance.

Angelina managed to break free and lunged at Daryl. Grabbing him by the leather coat, she used all her strength to push him up against the car.

"As far as I'm concerned, you have no respect. And if you don't get the hell out of here, I'm going to make sure you join my mother!"

Trevor grabbed Angelina by the waist and flung her body behind his. "Angelina, I'm sorry you feel that way, but you're acting like a crazed animal."

Pushing him off her, Angelina took a defiant stance and glared at Trevor. "You and your wife have disrespected me by bringing this piece of garbage to my mother's wake. I want you three to get the hell away from me!" she said before storming towards the funeral parlor.

The three stood there in silence until Angelina made her way inside.

"I told you it was a bad idea to bring him," Linda said.

"Don't tell me what to do. Daryl's my boy, and I'm behind him one hundred percent!" Trevor shot back.

Linda was about to respond, but Daryl managed to stand between the two.

"Hey, don't fight on my account. It was my idea to come. I wanted to show the bitch I was the bigger person, but I guess she don't appreciate all I've done for her. Hey, let's get in the car and go have some drinks. We need to celebrate the fact that I finished the sequel to *Betrayal*. When this book drops, I'm going to show Angelina that it will be just as successful without her help. She's going to be begging me to come back," Daryl commented with a sly smile.

Disgusted, Linda stormed towards Third Avenue. "Well, you two go celebrate. I'm taking a taxi home."

Trevor shrugged off Linda's statement and got in the car with Daryl.

*****

Angelina stormed past the stunned mourners as she made her way towards the back of the hallway. Realizing something was definitely wrong with her cousin, Jennie followed her.

"Angelina, are you alright?" Jennie asked, catching up to her by the restrooms.

"No. Do you believe Daryl showed up? He was about to walk in like everything's good," Angelina responded.

Jennie's pale cheeks turned red with rage. Jennie and Angelina had the same facial features, except Jennie's complexion was much lighter with natural dark blonde hair from her biological father's Jewish roots.

"That bastard had the nerve to show up here after what he

did to you? He's got some fucking nerve."

"Yeah, but thank God I was outside. If that bastard would have walked in here, it would've been war, Jennie," Angelina stated in an intense tone.

Jennie sat down on one of the plush chairs that adorned the small waiting area leading to the restroom. Having always been the calm one, she wanted desperately to ease her cousin's pain.

"I have an idea. Why don't you go away for a few weeks...head to Florida? You could spend time at Uncle Nelson's house. You know he won't mind, especially with all that has happened to you."

Nelson Velez was a common fixture at Taft Projects. He not only worked in the maintenance department of the complex, but he lived in the building next to Angelina's mother. He was also a well-respected numbers runner for the local Mafioso's on First Avenue and 116th Street.

Angelina loved him dearly. When her father ran off, Nelson immediately filled his shoes, becoming a father figure and taking Angelina under his wing. Back in those days, Ana was strapped for cash, so he would organize poker games four times a week at her home. He would give Ana enough cash to buy food for the games, and then while everyone was having a good time eating and playing cards, he passed around his housing hat for contributions to the "Ana and Angelina's Help Pay Our Bills Fund", as he called it. As Angelina grew to become a young woman, it was Nelson who paid for her schooling. He even paid for her wedding when she decided to marry at age nineteen.

It was no secret that Nelson had a number of different women, even though he was married with six children. His wife never intervened, though. Her Christian beliefs were strong, so divorce was not an option. She stayed dedicated to him and their kids. Ana was the only woman he never slept with. Although he found her attractive enough, they never wanted to ruin the friendship they shared.

114

By the time he retired, Nelson and his wife chose to stay married but live separate lives. He secured her a sprawling condominium on the Upper East Side, while he moved to Florida's Miami Estates where he purchased a mini mansion by the ocean. Despite moving three thousand miles away from New York, he kept in close contact with his unofficial adopted child.

"You know, Jennie, that sounds like a great idea," Angelina said, nodding her head. "I need to get the hell away from New York. Mami's gone and I need a change of scenery."

"That's right, girl. Take a couple of weeks, then come back and work for your friend Desire," Jennie replied with a smile.

Angelina smiled back at her favorite cousin. She had three other cousins, but Jennie had been the one she was always closest to. When Jennie's mother abandoned her, Ana's mother got full custody. In addition to her grandmother, Jennie's aunts Antonia and Ana helped raised her. So, the two women were more than cousins; they were sisters.

"I'm going to call Papi Nelson tonight so he can make the arrangements. He wanted to be here, but he had too much business to handle in Florida. Papi Nelson did make sure Mami had the best. He spoke to the funeral director personally and had everything taken care of. All I had to do was forward the insurance check," Angelina stated.

Every time she spoke of Nelson, she gushed like a little girl. She considered him the only father she knew.

"Uncle Nelson is the best. Go see him, cuz. He will take care of you." Jennie got up and hugged her favorite cousin tightly. "Everything's gonna be alright," she said softly as Angelina sobbed on her shoulder.

*****

The following day was as gloomy as the burial. Ana was

115

buried at Rose Hill Cemetery in Linden, New Jersey. It rained all morning up until Ana's remains were lowered into the ground. Then, suddenly, the sun broke through the clouds and beamed down on the plastic tent erected over the area where the mourners stood. Angelina considered it a defining moment. She felt her mother had finally found happiness after many years of heartache and had gone home.

The custom among Puerto Ricans was that after the burial, the family holds nine days of prayer at the home of the deceased. A curandera, usually a person who is a friend of the family, presides among the mourners and recites the prayers of the dead. They were prayers Angelina knew by heart from her many years of attending different resamientos, a series of prayers to the dead for nine days, as a child. Knowing all of this, Nelson booked Angelina's flight for her to leave New York on the tenth day.

When Flight 1085 left Laguardia Airport at 9 a.m., it was a bone-chilling twelve degrees in New York. When Angelina arrived at Ft. Lauderdale/Hollywood International Airport at 12:30 p.m., the temperature was ninety degrees and sunny. Angelina walked out the revolving doors of the airport's exit and immediately felt the stress leave her soul. It didn't take long for her to spot the driver dressed in black slacks and a white shirt holding a cardboard sign with the name "Rivera" written in black ink.

When Angelina arrived at Nelson's home, she was informed that he was out running errands, but he left specific instructions for his household staff to make Angelina as comfortable as possible. As soon as she walked through the double wood oak doors of the residence, three housekeepers were waiting to take her bags to the upstairs bedroom. Angelina looked around in awe at the fabulous layout of the mansion. It had a huge foyer at the entrance with a large circular glass table in the middle, and sprawling circular staircases leading up to the second story adorned each side of the house. It reminded her of Tony Montana's house from the

116

movie *Scarface*.

Her bedroom was just as amazing. Designed in the old Spaniard style, it was furnished with a king-sized bed covered in silk sheets and had a soft net draped over each side. On the south side of the room were bay doors that led to a small balcony that overlooked the huge swimming pool by the ocean. Angelina was too exhausted to fully appreciate all of the beautiful views that surrounded her at the moment. Instead, she removed her clothes and snuggled onto the plush bed to take a much-needed nap.

When she awoke, it was 6:00 p.m. While she slept, the housekeepers had put her clothes away in a walk-in closet. On the Victorian-style loveseat, she noticed a yellow sundress and a pair of slip-on sandals that Nelson had apparently purchased for her. She quickly showered and dressed, letting her hair flow she ran down the steps toward the den where she knew he would be. Nelson purchased his home a year after Angelina moved back to New York, so she never got to see the mansion in person. However, he had sent her pictures of his home. Therefore, she was familiar with the layout and knew where to find his favorite room.

Without knocking, she opened the door to find Nelson sitting behind his glass desk reviewing some documents. The smoke from his Cuban cigar disappeared slowly into the air. He looked up and smiled as Angelina rushed towards him. He sprung up from his leather chair with extended arms as he lovingly greeted her.

"Baby, how are you? I'm so glad you're here," he said, his baby blue eyes gleaming with delight.

"Papi, I'm so glad to see you! I missed you so much," Angelina responded, trying not to get too emotional.

"Well, you're here with me now. I promised your mother I would take care of you and I will," he told her.

Angelina felt safe in his arms. He was her driving force. Releasing herself from his embrace, she looked at him and smiled.

"Papi, you have not changed a bit."

"Well, you sure have. You are more beautiful than ever, my child," he replied fondly.

Nelson was a tall, stocky man who looked more Irish than Puerto Rican with his light skin and fire red hair. For a man of seventy-nine years, the gods had been kind to him; he didn't have one wrinkle on his face.

"Are you hungry?" he asked.

"I'm starving. Where we going?"

"I'm gonna take you to a great restaurant. We'll talk there," Nelson replied as he stroked Angelina's hair.

Once in his limousine, they headed to Joe's Stone Crab on Washington Street in Miami Beach. The restaurant opened its doors when the stone crabs were in season. Many celebrities, including Ricky Martin and P. Diddy who considered Miami Beach their second home, frequently visited it. Nelson was such a frequent visitor that he had his favorite table reserved, right by the bay windows overlooking Miami Beach's skyline. A bottle of Dom Pérignon was at his table with two crystal-stemmed glasses filled to the rim, and the crabs were cooking in the kitchen's steamer. They were Nelson's favorite twosome.

As they admired the full moon shining over the warm water's soft waves, Nelson observed Angelina's face with concern.

"So how are you doing, sweetie?" he asked.

Angelina shrugged her shoulders while taking a sip of her champagne. "I'm okay, Papi. I still can't believe Mami's gone, though."

"Mamita, you know your mother's been sick. It was her time," he replied.

"But, I feel like it's my fault. If I wouldn't have gotten in trouble, she would still be alive today," she replied softly, tears streaming down her cheeks.

Nelson rested his hand on hers. "Listen, it wasn't your fault. You were a good daughter to her considering the way you grew up. God knows I tried to let your mother know her drinking would catch up with her in her later years. Mamita, I saw firsthand the pain you went through growing up. Your father was gone, and Ana drowned in the liquor so much that she practically left you to care for yourself. That's why my wife and I stepped in. We knew you may have ended up on the wrong side of the street if we hadn't. But, we all make mistakes. I hope you don't hate your mother for hers."

"No, Papi. She did the best she could with what she had. I just feel like I have no one to turn to now," Angelina said.

"You have me. I will be here for you no matter what."

Nelson paused their conversation when the waiter approached with the stone crab legs. They took their silver crackers and began to break open the hard shells.

"So your mother told me you had problems with some guy in New York. What happened?" he asked as he dug into the shell with his small fork.

Angelina went on to tell him about Daryl.

"Well, you know what they say. What goes around comes around, and he's gonna get his," Nelson said in disgust.

He was noticeably angry at the story he'd just heard.

"I just feel used. Damn, I feel like a fool, Papi. He ruined my life. I just want to forget about him, but I can't. He even tried to discredit me with people I built relationships with in the book game. I'm glad Desire is giving me a chance, though. She is really nice and confident I can do a great job," Angelina shared.

"Well, while you're here, I'm going to make sure you enjoy yourself. I set aside my business dealings so I can dedicate the whole two weeks to you. I'm going to show you a good time, okay?"

His smile made everything better instantly.

"Okay, Papi. Thank you so much for everything."

It felt good to be able to smile for a change, something she hadn't done much of lately.

Nelson did not disappoint. Angelina spent her days

working on her suntan by the pool and her evenings visiting the various clubs of South Beach. He had VIP status everywhere they went. During her last weekend in Miami, he hired a private plane so they could fly to Key West, where they cruised up and down Duval Street and watched the sun set while walking along the small beach by the hotel. She swore she could see the flickering lights from the island of Cuba from the shoreline.

At the end of her trip, Angelina arrived at Ft. Lauderdale Airport with a heavy heart. She didn't want to leave Miami, but she knew there was a lot to do back in New York. She had a new job to return to as well as continuing to take care of Ana's affairs. Although her name was on the lease, Angelina didn't want to stay in the apartment where she had suffered much pain. So, she had requested a transfer to a smaller apartment on the West Side. She longed for a fresh start.

As she passed one of the newsstands by the terminal, she glanced at the various newspapers from different states. Angelina stopped in her tracks when she saw the front page of New York's leading newspaper. It displayed a picture of DeeDee and Daryl, with a headline that read: *Young Woman Killed; Local Author Held as Person of Interest.*

Angelina couldn't believe it. DeeDee was dead!

Chapter 12
Time To Face The Music

Daryl nervously paced back and forth in his bedroom while puffing on his third blunt. He'd been smoking non-stop since returning from West Harlem's 32nd Precinct, where they had held him in a small, dark room for twenty-four hours questioning him about DeeDee's murder. One of the detectives, Arturo Sanchez, was a real bastard, screaming in Daryl's ear about how he should confess and get it over with. Daryl wanted to snap the motherfucker's fat neck every time he walked back in the room, but he maintained his composure and kept his mouth shut as he stared into space without a care. He had been in similar situations before and knew how the system worked. Daryl was confident they only had circumstantial evidence or, in other words, hearsay.

Upon his release, Daryl arrived home to a mob of reporters waiting in front of his building. When word got out that the person of interest was an urban writer, the media flocked to see if they could get a statement from the "local celebrity". Daryl had to park his car three blocks away and crawl through his bedroom window to avoid the frenzy.

"This shit is crazy!" he told Trevor.

"I know. I had to dodge reporters again as I walked in the building. Those muthafuckas are like parasites," Trevor said, taking a sip of cognac.

"I can't go outside, dawg, and I'm going fuckin' crazy in

here! Mommy's with my sister, and I'm here alone. My attorney says it should die down soon, but when?" Daryl asked, as if his friend had the answer.

"I don't know what to tell you. This is a serious situation you're in. Murder is no joke," Trevor replied.

"I should've never have fucked around with that bitch. 'Cause of her I lost Angelina. I lost credibility with book stores, too! They don't wanna fuck with my book. They say readers don't wanna buy books from a guy who murdered a pregnant woman. But, I didn't do it!" Daryl cried out.

Trevor walked over to Daryl. Placing his hand on his boy's shoulder, he tried to calm him down.

"Dawg, you've been my friend since we were kids, and I want you to be honest with me. Did you kill that hoe?" he asked in a soft voice.

Daryl pulled away from him in anger. "Damn, I just told you I didn't do it! I thought if anyone would believe me, it would be you. I swear I didn't kill the bitch!"

"I'm just asking, 'cause you changed ever since you started fucking around with that girl. I remember our hustling days and know what you're capable of doing for the almighty dollar, but you were never greedy and never let any hoe get in the way of your flow. You were out of control."

"What the fuck do you mean?" Daryl asked.

"Daryl, what the hell were you thinking when you recorded yourself fucking DeeDee and that other chick? Especially when you knew DeeDee would use it against you!" Trevor shot back.

"That's just it; I didn't know the bitch would send it to Angelina. I thought I had her under control," Daryl replied.

"Well, I guess you were wrong, my brotha, 'cause she not only showed it to Angelina, but she was bold enough to confront her. On top of that, she trapped you by getting pregnant. Didn't you use a condom?" Trevor asked.

"The bitch told me that she was on the pill," Daryl said in a desperate attempt to justify his poor judgement.

Trevor chuckled lightly. "And you believed her? When any bitch says she's on the pill, you need to back it up with a condom."

Daryl sat on the edge of his bed with his shoulders slumped. He felt defeated. "Damn, dawg, you're right. I let the success of my book go to my head so much that I stopped taking care of business. Now I'm about to lose everything."

"Look, you need to calm down. You'll see how the reporters will move on to the next story. Once everything blows over, you can pick up where you left off with your books," Trevor told him.

"I've done too much damage already," Daryl responded, feeling dejected as he took another hit of his blunt.

*****

Angelina finally arrived at the place she had called home for as long as she could remember. Although surrounded by familiar furnishings, the atmosphere seemed totally different. There was an eerie silence without the sound of Ana's favorite soap operas blaring from her bedroom. The aroma of rice and beans that once filled the apartment was gone. Her mother was gone.

Shaking off the strong desire to cry, Angelina placed her suitcase by the door and began going through the mountain of mail Jennie had placed on the small table by the foyer. Her phone rang, interrupting her.

"Hello?"

"Hi, Angelina. It's Linda. You probably don't want to talk to me, but I just wanted to make sure you're okay. I've been trying to contact you for the past two weeks. Is everything alright?"

"Hey, girl. Yes, I'm okay. Just got in from the airport. I took a trip to Florida. But, I'm glad you called. I wanted to apologize for my outburst towards you and Trevor at the funeral home. I realized you probably didn't intentionally bring Daryl. I know he has a way of convincing people to do things that are out of pocket," Angelina said.

"I know. I asked Trevor not to bring him, but you know how it is. Those two have defended each other since childhood. But, trust me, Trevor feels just as bad. Tell you what, why don't you come by the house and we can talk more? I'm dying to see you," Linda pleaded.

Angelina hesitated for a bit before responding.

"Daryl's not gonna be there, right?"

"Oh no! I wouldn't do that to you, girl. Anyway, he doesn't want to deal with the reporters outside his house. Come on, we'll order pizza and talk."

"Okay, I'll be there in an hour," Angelina told her.

It took no time for Angelina to freshen up and head out the door. While standing on the corner of 115th Street and Fifth Avenue to hail a cab, she couldn't help but look towards Daryl's neighborhood where the news vans nearly blocked off traffic heading towards the westside. There were reporters outside with cameras and microphones ready to capture any glimpse of Daryl. It looked like a zoo.

Shifting her focus to the oncoming traffic, she was about to hail the first available taxi, when she noticed a black Lincoln Town Car approaching her. At first, she thought it was a gypsy cab but then realized it was a detective's vehicle. She watched as a burly Hispanic male got out of the driver's side and walked towards her. His dark gray suit and shades fit the appearance of a detective perfectly.

"Good afternoon, Ms. Rivera. My name is Detective Arturo Sanchez, and I need to ask you some questions regarding Denise Richardson and Daryl James," he informed her.

"There isn't much I can tell you, detective. I know little about Ms. Richardson, and Mr. James and I are no longer together," she answered dryly.

"Yes, I'm aware that you and Mr. James are no longer together. However, there is an ongoing murder investigation, and we are gathering information from people who knew them."

"Yes, I heard of Ms. Richardson's untimely death, and I am truly sorry to hear that," Angelina replied.

"Are you really? Word on the street is that you two had a huge argument when you found out they were having an affair. It must have been very painful for you," Detective Sanchez stated smugly.

Angelina glared at the detective. She wanted to give him a piece of her mind but managed to remain poised.

"Listen, I don't know what you heard, but what happened between Ms. Richardson and I is no one's business," she replied.

"When it involves a homicide, whatever surrounds the circumstances is the NYPD's business," he shot back.

Growing tired of Detective Sanchez's taunting remarks, Angelina wanted to end the conversation before she told him to go to hell.

"Unless you're going to arrest me, I suggest you let me go on my way," she replied, standing her ground.

Her fiery attitude and voluptuous body turned the detective on. He couldn't help but admire how her Calvin Klein wool coat hugged her full breasts, a feature Detective Sanchez loved in a woman.

"I'm not gonna arrest you, but I would like for you to come down to the precinct and answer a few questions. By the way, your tan looks great. Were you in the Bahamas?" he inquired.

"Well, if you must know, I was in Miami for two weeks. I have the plane tickets and receipts to prove it," she said.

"It's not necessary. Here's my card. Call me tomorrow and we'll set up a time okay?" He extended his business card towards her.

Angelina took his card and watched as he casually walked back to his car and drove off. Tucking his card into her coat pocket, she hailed a cab and continued on to her destination.

*****

Linda warmly greeted Angelina at the door.

"Hey, girl, it's good to see you. Damn, you got a killer tan!" she said in admiration.

"Thanks. I haven't felt this good in a long time," Angelina expressed as she walked into the house. She removed her coat, threw it over the arm of her friend's couch, and took a seat at the kitchen table while Linda stood at the counter preparing a garden salad. The sweet aroma of the pizza in the oven made Angelina realize she was really hungry.

"So how was Florida?" Linda asked.

"Oh my God, it was great! I had so much fun. It was hard for me to leave," Angelina replied.

"I'm glad, girl. God knows you needed to get away from New York, especially after all that has happened," Linda said with a sigh.

"Yes, Florida was the best medicine. It was just what I needed. But, as soon as I got home, drama reared its ugly head again. What's the deal with this murder that's been all over the news?" Angelina asked.

"Girl, it happened last week. That girl was sweating Daryl bad. She kept harassing him about how he had to marry her because she was pregnant."

This news hit Angelina like a punch to her stomach.

"Wait, Linda. She was pregnant?"

Realizing Angelina didn't know, Linda put down the kitchen knife and sat next to her.

"Yes, girl, she was pregnant. It was all over the papers. Didn't you read it?" Linda asked.

"I saw the headline on the front of one of the newspapers at the airport, but I didn't buy it. I figured the less I knew about it the better. I can't believe Daryl," Angelina replied in total shock.

Linda looked at her suspiciously. "Angelina, you don't

think he murdered that girl, do you?"

"As much as I hate him, I can't imagine him being a killer. I'm just disappointed he thought about having a baby with her. He knew my biggest regret was not being able to have a child. He would tell me over and over it didn't matter because he had Angel and didn't want any more kids. I guess it's just one more of Daryl's lies," Angelina replied somberly.

"No, it wasn't like that. From what Trevor told me, the pregnancy was not planned. You know how these chickenheads are; they get pregnant to try to keep a man."

Angelina felt so much anguish in her heart. She didn't want to hear any more about DeeDee's pregnancy. All she wanted to do was change the subject quickly.

"Well, some detective wants to see me tomorrow about DeeDee's murder."

"Are you going to see him?" Linda asked.

Angelina sighed. "I'll have to go. You know how these cops are. If you don't go, they'll harass you."

Linda nodded in agreement. "True that."

"Well, I do have some good news. I have another job. I connected with a well-known publisher named Desire, and she gave me a job working in her sales/marketing department."

Linda's eyes widened with delight. "You mean Desire of Paradise Publishing?"

Angelina nodded as she took a sip of her iced tea.

"Desire is my girl! I've read all her books. She's on fire! Her books have been some of the best I've ever read," Linda replied, sounding excited.

"Yes, she is. We met at Riker's. She's been a great friend ever since."

Angelina's sadness resurfaced at the thought of her stay at Riker's. She still blamed herself for her mother's demise.

Sensing her friend's grief, Linda gently held her hand.

"Angelina, what happened to your mother was not your fault."

"I can't help but feel that if I were there, my mom would still be alive," Angelina replied as tears gathered in the corners of her eyes.

"Look, with time, you'll realize it was just her time," Linda stated, hoping her words would comfort her friend.

"Funny, my dad told me the same thing. I wish I could believe it."

Linda looked at her with a confused expression. "I thought your dad abandoned you as a child? Did you find him?"

Angelina chuckled softly. "Not my biological dad. Papi Nelson is my unofficial adopted father. He was there for me when my dad left."

As Linda served the pizza and salad, she listened while Angelina told her about her trip to Miami and how Nelson was so important to her.

*****

The next morning, Angelina walked into the 32nd Precinct for her meeting with Detective Sanchez. As she entered the doors, memories of her arrest swirled inside her like a tidal wave. Her nerves were shot and her body trembled. She tucked her hands in her coat pockets to hide her sweaty palms. Taking a deep breath, she slowly approached the front desk where a uniformed police officer sat on a high wooden chair reading a newspaper. He was a white guy in his 50's with balding grey hair. The deep wrinkles around his tired blue eyes showed how years on the beat had taken its toll.

Sensing her presence, the police officer lowered his newspaper just enough to focus his baby blues.

"May I help you?"

"I have an appointment with Detective Sanchez. My name is Angelina Rivera," she politely replied.

He stared at her for a few seconds, then placed his newspaper on the old wooden desk in front of him before

128

grabbing the receiver of an old-fashioned phone next to him. As Angelina scoped out the lobby, he proceeded to dial some numbers.

"Hey, Sanchez, you have someone here to see you. She says her name is Angelina Rivera."

Words were exchanged and his attention returned to her.

"He'll be down in a few minutes. Have a seat," he scruffed as he hung up the receiver and pointed toward a steel bench at the other end of the room. Angelina respectfully acknowledged his instruction.

While waiting, Angelina stared at the large NYPD insignia on the opposite wall. The blue and gray pigments showed signs of aging as chips of paint peeled off the concrete walls. Even the precinct's number had faded into the gray canvas that covered the wall. Once again, her mind wandered to her days at Riker's Island. All of her life, she encountered nothing but downfalls, but she realized her biggest downfall was the day she met Daryl James. Many men had broken her heart; however, Daryl's betrayal was the worst she had ever experienced. Angelina's pain was mixed with anger. Not at Daryl, but with herself. She let her pain consume her to the point of driving her to the bottle and subsequently to jail.

A slight tap on her shoulder interrupted Angelina's train of thought.

"Ms. Rivera, are you okay?" she heard a man's voice ask.

When she looked up, Detective Sanchez was standing over her with a puzzled look on his face.

"Yes, I'm okay," she replied, quickly standing up.

"Okay. Well, first, I'd like to thank you for taking the time to come and see me. Let's go upstairs so we can talk privately." He motioned her towards the elevators.

When the elevator arrived at the 6th floor, the detective squad area was bustling with men and women getting ready to start their day shifts. She was surprised to see how undercover detectives looked and dressed like the street thugs that roamed her neighborhood. Back in the 1980's, no matter how much a cop tried to blend in with the crowd, everyone could tell he or she was 5-0. She recalled one of her good friends who hustled on the streets telling her that the best way to tell a D.T. was by the shoes he wore and the way he walked. Nowadays, this new breed of law enforcement could walk up to a dealer and get whatever they wanted. The only thing that set them apart from the street thugs was the badge that hung from the silver chain around their necks.

A few men stopped their conversation mid-sentence to stare at Angelina as she followed Detective Sanchez across the room. She looked stunning in her black and white Marc Jacobs tweed coat and Manolo Blahnik stilettos, a gift from her Uncle Nelson.

"May I take your coat?" Detective Sanchez asked.

He, too, was mesmerized by her beauty and poise. He felt his heart start to beat faster as she removed her coat, revealing the black knit dress that perfectly hugged every inch of her curves.

Coughing a bit to retain his composure, he pointed towards the chair next to his desk.

"Please have a seat," he said nervously. "Would you like some coffee?"

"No, thank you. I'd just like to get this over with," Angelina replied, placing her coat on her lap.

Unfazed by her impatience, he sat behind his desk and opened a large manila folder. "I called you in because we need to tie up any loose ends pertaining to this investigation. We need to understand the events that led up to Ms. Richardson's murder."

"Well, I don't know how I can be of any help. As I told you yesterday, I knew little about Ms. Richardson," Angelina responded.

"Yes, I know. You two met when she informed you that she and Daryl were…having a fling," he stated in a tone that showed he had no compassion for the hurt Angelina suffered as a result of Daryl's infidelity.

Angelina stared at the detective, her patience wearing thin. "Look, you and I know that I don't have to be here answering your questions. Whatever happened to Dee...I mean, Denise Richardson has nothing to do with me. I was in Florida at the time of the murder. Yes, Daryl and I had a relationship, but he and I are no longer together. So, if you think I'm going to sit here and allow you to flaunt the facts of Daryl's affair in my face, you have another thing coming."

Detective Sanchez didn't take kindly to her non-cooperation. "Daryl played you like a violin, then threw you away when you were no longer fun to play with. We gathered a lot of evidence in his room, including the X-rated DVD that he and Denise participated in while in Atlanta. We also know of the pregnancy. Daryl James is a piece of shit ex-drug dealer who's now trying to lead people to believe he's legit 'cause he wrote a book!"

Angelina shot up from her chair and began putting on her coat. "If you're done questioning me, I'd like to go home. I have things to do."

Detective Sanchez slowly rose from his chair. "There are no more questions, Ms. Rivera. I'm sorry if I agitated you. I also know of your mother's passing. My condolences."

"If you have any further questions, I would appreciate it if you let me know ahead of time so I can come in with my attorney," she shot back before storming towards the elevator.

Detective Sanchez watched as her hips swayed with defiance yet at the same time seductively.

Damn, that woman is fine! What the fuck did she ever see in that piece of shit Daryl James? he thought to himself as he sat down to inspect the contents of the folder.

Chapter 13
Harlem Is Burning

Angelina sat on the stone bench by her mother's grave absorbing the peace and quiet surrounding the huge cemetery. The yellow orchids, Ana's favorite, were perched in a crystal vase and gently swayed in the unseasonably warm winds that engulfed New York City in January. Sadness filled her heart as she remembered how one year earlier her mother's body had been lowered into the very ground where those orchids stood. Angelina thought about how much had changed since her mother's demise. Gone was the Angelina who held on to a relationship regardless of how badly she was treated in hopes that her significant other would change. She was now her own person devoted to loving herself first. The roads that led to her newfound feeling were not easy ones.

Upon her return from Florida, she spent the first two months sorting out keepsakes at her mother's place. Unable to take all of Ana's belongings to her new one-bedroom apartment, Angelina donated them along with her clothes to The Salvation Army; she figured another family could benefit from them. In the meantime, she appeared in court and was found guilty of the DWI. With it only being her first offense, her license was suspended for six months, and she was ordered to do ten days of community service in addition to attending a mandatory DWI class and Alcoholics Anonymous meetings for the following three months. At first, she hated the idea of bearing her soul to total strangers, but as she continued going, she found they had the same fears she did. With every visit, she connected with them more.

During that whole time, Desire proved to be a true friend. She kept Angelina busy while teaching her all about the business. Angelina was amazed at how much information Daryl had kept from her. He limited her to making phone calls and collecting the money, unlike Desire who pushed Angelina into the spotlight. Desire even had Angelina working at her bookstand selling books. Angelina was eager to learn every aspect of the book game. She could still remember her first day; her palms were sweaty and she struggled with her words whenever a customer approached the table. Desire was very patient with her, though.

What a difference a year makes. Angelina was now a very confident woman who hustled books like the best of them. She even changed her appearance, opting for a short bob haircut and wearing sexier clothing.

While Angelina's life flourished, Daryl's became a nightmare. The notoriety of his indirect involvement in DeeDee's murder along with his arrogant behavior killed his booming book sales. Still considered a person of interest, he was constantly harassed by the detectives of the 32nd Precinct. They constantly hauled him in for questioning whenever a so-called lead would pop up. However, since the gun used to kill DeeDee had not been found, they couldn't hold him. That didn't stop them from giving Daryl a very hard time, though.

His lack of experience in sales was evident when vendors along with bookstores refused to put up with his many blowups. He would bark at them, demanding they purchase his book, and then harass them when they'd refuse. One day, he threatened to topple a street vendor's table when the African man refused to purchase his books at two dollars under his usual wholesale price. He was becoming more and more desperate.

Wearing out his welcome in New York, he decided to

showcase his books in Philadelphia. He was good friends with a few bookstore owners there and hoped the sequel to *Betrayal* would blow up in sales. Daryl quickly finished writing his second novel and shipped the finished manuscript to the printers. Hearing how Angelina was doing well, he had a personal vendetta against her. He wanted to prove to her that he was still on top.

What a disaster that turned out to be. The editing for his book was poor, and the cover was the worst cut-and-paste job anyone had ever seen. It looked like it had been done by a two-year-old. When the reviewers got hold of a copy, it was slammed and he was labeled an incompetent writer. Daryl became the laughing stock of the urban literary industry.

Unable to defeat Angelina in the publishing world, Daryl took what money he had left from his book sales and purchased two bricks of pure cocaine, returning to his life as a drug dealer. He knew crack was still in high demand, so he recruited Budda to move his product when Trevor refused. Within months, he was moving crack all over Taft and Foster Projects, as well as DeeDee's old neighborhood on Lenox Avenue thanks to Butta Face's connections.

Angelina stood up from the bench and moved closer to the headstone bearing her mother's name. She gently stroked the limestone before kissing the cold rock.

"Well, Mami, I gotta go. As I promised you on the day you died, I brought your favorite flowers on the anniversary of your death. I miss you, Mami, but I now realize you are in a better place; a place where no one can hurt you."

With those words, Angelina got in her car and drove off.

*****

By the time she got home, Angelina was in good spirits. She had a big night ahead of her. Desire was launching her latest novel with a huge party at her favorite neighborhood lounge on 108th Street between Lexington and Third Avenue.

Not one for fancy parties, Desire preferred holding her events in the neighborhood where she grew up. "Keep it Hood" she would always say.

Angelina grew excited as she thought about getting the opportunity to finally meet some big publishers and authors from out of town.

Desire wanted her to look perfect, so she took Angelina shopping. Against Angelina's wishes, Desire picked out a pair of black leather pants with matching bustier and leather spiked heel boots with fringes that ran along her calves. The sterling silver handcuff necklace added the finishing touch. When Angelina finished putting on her outfit, she felt like a different woman, not only on the inside but on the outside too.

Opting for a cab, Angelina arrived at the lounge promptly at 7:00 p.m. Desire instructed her staff to arrive one hour earlier to prepare for her guests. They had spent the previous night decorating the lounge with huge posters of each book Desire had written. A poster of her latest book was perched on the wall behind the small stage where a long table draped in a black tablecloth showcased copies of her book. Desire knew how to organize a party; she had beautiful women dressed in black satin shorts and tight t-shirts at the entrance to greet guests with small goody bags filled with cosmetics, perfumes, and a copy of her book. Desire herself looked lovely wearing a black pantsuit with a V-neck cut down to her navel.

"It's about time you got here! I'm nervous and needed you here," Desire barked.

Angelina smiled as she followed her inside. Many people thought of Desire as being arrogant, demanding, and even a pain in the ass. They may have been right, but the one thing they could not say about her was that she was a fake friend. She would tell you the truth to your face without batting an eyelash, and when you became her friend, it was for life.

The elite who's who showed up to show support.

Angelina was introduced to so many people that she felt drunk with happiness although she hadn't touched a drink. While Angelina talked business with bookstore owners and vendors, Desire signed her books. Many who knew Angelina before her transformation walked over to her and complimented her wardrobe and new hairstyle; they were floored at how good she looked. Halfway through the evening, Angelina had collected about one hundred business cards from all who were interested in getting Desire's new book on their shelf.

Once Desire finished signing her books, she walked over to the microphone at the end of the stage and began to speak.

"Hello, everyone. First of all, I'd like to thank you all for coming…"

Angelina was so focused on Desire's speech she didn't notice a male figure creeping up behind her.

"What's up, Angelina?" the familiar voice whispered in her ear.

She quickly spun around and found herself face to face with the man who ruined her life.

"What the hell are you doing here, Daryl?" she asked in a stern voice.

"Damn, baby, you look fine as hell. I kinda regret leaving you," he replied in his usual cocky tone.

"If I remember correctly, I left you. But, it doesn't matter. As you can see, I've moved on," Angelina said.

Daryl chuckled. "I see you have. Well, to answer your question, I heard your boss was having a party. So, I figured I'd show up to improve the ambiance of this joint."

"Ambiance? Now that's a big word for you," she retorted.

Her last comment angered him. "Oh, so now you a big woman 'cause you working with Desire. You and I know if I wanna tap that ass, I could. You don't have to pretend 'cause your peeps is here."

Angelina let out a cheerful chuckle. "You would be the last man who would tap this, honey. I'm not the same person

137

you met and you need to know that."

Engrossed in her argument with Daryl, Angelina hadn't noticed that Desire had finished her speech and was storming towards them.

"What the fuck are you doing here, Daryl?" she growled.

"Damn, Desire, is that any way to greet your paid guest?" he asked.

"I will gladly give you a refund and kick your ass out." Desire then turned to Angelina. "Is he bothering you? 'Cause if he is, I'll make sure he doesn't walk out on his own."

As much as she would have loved to see Daryl get kicked out on his ass, she didn't want any of her drama to ruin the party.

"No, Desire. As long as he stays away from me, we're cool."

For the rest of the evening, Angelina made it a point to avoid being within inches of Daryl. She kept busy making sure the other guests were having a good time. Daryl made every lame attempt to hang around the other authors bragging about how much money he had. At one point, he mentioned how he kept a safe with about eighty thousand dollars for emergencies. Most authors at the party made twice as much in advances from publishers who were itching to get them on their team. It would have been a good idea if Daryl had researched the authors on Google so he knew the company he was amongst.

It was after midnight and the party was still going strong. Having had a few glasses of chardonnay, Desire began dancing in the center of the dance floor with the other guests. Angelina thought it a safe time to have a glass of wine herself. She had sworn off hard liquor but still enjoyed the occasional glass of fermented grapes.

As she enjoyed her wine, Angelina was startled when the front door flung open and Detective Sanchez entered the lounge with eight uniformed police officers trailing behind him. They walked past the crowd of partygoers until

Detective Sanchez spotted Daryl sitting on one of the plush chairs opposite the deejay booth.

"Daryl James?" Detective Sanchez asked.

"You know who I am, asshole," Daryl answered sarcastically as he stood up.

Detective Sanchez quickly slammed him against the wall and slapped the silver handcuffs on Daryl's wrists. Daryl squirmed in an attempt to turn around, but he was no match for the cops who surrounded him.

"What the fuck are you doing?" Daryl asked.

"Daryl James, you are hereby placed under arrest for the murder of Denise Richardson. You have the right to remain silent. Anything you say can and will be used against you…"

Angelina stood watching in shock as the detective pushed Daryl out the door.

Chapter 14
His World Crumbled

Daryl sat on the cold bench staring at the thick bars in front of him. It was a slow night at the precinct, so he was fingerprinted and processed soon after arriving. The last time he was pinched was a walk in the park. But now, he was being accused of murder, and the thought of spending the rest of his life in jail made him sick to his stomach. He thought about not being able to ever see his daughter Angel again and not being there for his mother if she ever got sick. For some reason, he also thought about what Angelina would think of him if, in fact, they found him guilty.

He felt a sorrowful knot build in his throat until he heard heavy footsteps approachig his cell. He quickly swallowed his pain and sat upright.

"We're gonna take you downtown in about a half hour," Detective Sanchez told him as he leaned against the wall directly across from the cell.

"Whatever," Daryl snapped. "I need to make a phone call to make sure my lawyer is at the courthouse."

Detective Sanchez laughed. "That's going to be a waste of time. You ain't getting no bail, my brotha."

Daryl wanted to grab him by the neck and squeeze until the smirk disappeared from his face.

"So do I get my phone call or what?" he asked in a thunderous voice.

Detective Sanchez's smile faded as he stared coldly at him. "You will get your fucking phone call when we are ready, asshole," he replied before storming off.

Staring at the steel bars, Daryl dug his fingernails into the palm of his hands until he broke the skin. The blood dripped as his anger grew.

*****

The squad car made its way east on 116th Street towards FDR Drive. Daryl stared out the window silently as the car passed by Sam's Pizza Shop where he took Angelina on their first date. For months, Daryl didn't bother getting his pizzas there, fearing he would run into her.

Heading south on FDR Drive, he glanced at the high-rise buildings to his left, an indication they were close to Central Booking. He solemnly stared at the East River. Daylight was approaching as the last rays of the moon danced on the murky waters below. A knot formed in Daryl's stomach as thoughts darted through his mind of not being able to see that view ever again.

The Manhattan Detention Center, also known as The Tombs, was located in the famous Chinatown area. Also awaiting their fate was anything and everything the NYPD had picked up that evening. There were drunks, drug dealers, prostitutes, and all the other lowlifes one could ever come across. After being taken into the facility, it took another four hours before Daryl was finally able to speak to his lawyer.

"So what's up?" Daryl asked.

Harvey Stein adjusted his glasses before skimming through the documents outlining all the charges against Daryl.

"I have to tell you, Mr. James, it doesn't look good for you. First of all, they have the murder weapon. Seems there was a homeless man fishing off the East River on 112th Street, when the weapon hooked onto his fishing line. He panicked and flagged down a police car that was cruising by, and like a Good Samaritan, he turned it in."

Daryl slammed his fist on the metal table, startling his attorney. "What the fuck does that have to do with me? They can't prove that gun is mine!" he growled.

Attorney Stein nervously shuffled through the papers before continuing. "The serial numbers on the gun matched a gun stolen from a store in Connecticut. When the detectives spoke to the gun dealer, he cracked and confessed that he sold a gun to an African American man named Leroy Perry, who is also known as Budda. He then reported it stolen just in case the gun was ever involved in any kind of illegal shooting. When they brought Mr. Perry in for questioning, he admitted to selling the gun to you for four hundred and fifty dollars. There are affidavits from several witnesses, including the deceased girl's cousin, stating the gun was in fact yours. Once they ran the ballistics, they concluded it was the same gun that killed Ms. Richardson."

"Butta Face? You mean to tell me that bitch talked to da cops, too!" Daryl was furious.

Attorney Stein nodded. "Yes. Now this is what we're going to do. Since the gun spent enough time underwater, the cops know they can't get any fingerprints off of it. The only thing they got is the word of a small-time drug dealer and small-time people I can easily discredit if we go to trial. When we're in front of the judge, of course, you will plead not guilty. I'm going to try to get your charges reduced to manslaughter so you can get bail by your next court date. You've been released from parole for some time now, so bail should be easy to get; that is, if they reduce the charges. In the meantime, sit tight and don't talk to anyone until our next court date."

"Okay, whatever you say." Daryl clasped his fingers together. "Do what you gotta do. Just get me outta here. I didn't kill that bitch!"

*****

Once in court, Daryl was officially charged with first-degree murder. The judge looked on in disgust as the prosecutor read the charges and details of the murder, rolling his eyes as they stated the victim was six weeks pregnant. He did not hesitate to deny bail and set the next court hearing for two weeks from that day.

When Daryl was taken to a holding cell, he immediately grabbed the phone posted on the wall and called the only person who could give him the comfort he needed.

"Hi, Mommy," he said.

Ramona immediately started crying uncontrollably as she screamed, "My baby! Oh Jesus, my baby!"

"Mommy, please don't cry. I need you to be strong. I'm gonna get outta this, okay?" he said, fighting to hold back his own tears.

Once Ramona calmed down, she told Daryl what had happened on her end.

"They came here with a search warrant and demolished my apartment. I kept asking them what they were looking for, but they just kept telling me to shut up and go sit in the living room. They were here for about three hours! I was so scared. Then I got a call from some detective informing me that you were arrested for murder. What the hell is going on, Daryl?" she asked, sounding frantic.

"Mommy, calm down. They're saying I murdered DeeDee. They must've gone to your house while I was at the party. Those motherfuckers picked me up in the middle of the festivities," he explained.

"Which party?" she asked.

"It was Desire's party that she threw for the launching of her new book," he responded solemnly.

For a few seconds, there was only silence on the other end of the phone.

"Why did you go to that party? You knew Angelina

would be there, baby. Haven't you caused her enough pain?"

"I haven't caused her a damn thing! I just wanted to get with some people who I knew would be there 'cause I want to get another book out and need to get reacquainted with people in the industry," he replied, using a harsh tone.

"Look, boy, you can't fool me. I know you still love Angelina, but you have to accept that you fucked up with her. I'm pissed at you for spreading lies about her. You can't imagine how bad I felt after all those bad things I said about her. I can't even look at her now because I'm too embarrassed. You have told one lie after another, Daryl, and I can't believe anything you say anymore. But, the only thing I can be sure of is that you're not a killer."

A wave of relief washed through Daryl's body.

"Mommy, I'm glad you don't think of me as a murderer. My lawyer is gonna call you tomorrow 'cause I have to go back to court in two weeks and he's gonna try to get my charges reduced to manslaughter so I can get out on bail. I'll need you to go to the bank and take all of the money out of the safe deposit box for me."

"Okay, baby. Just don't get into any trouble while you're in there, you hear?"

"Oh and another thing, if Butta Face or Budda ask how I'm doing, don't tell them anything. They're nothing but snitches!"

Chapter 15
Amazing Grace

Attorney Stein did exactly what he got paid to do. He convinced the District Attorney to reduce Daryl's charges. With there only being circumstantial evidence, manslaughter was the only thing they could charge him with. As his attorney predicted, the murky waters of the East River had washed away any fingerprints on the gun. Bail was set at twenty thousand dollars, and thanks to the money he had saved in his safe deposit box, he was released that afternoon with a return court date.

In the weeks that followed, Daryl stayed busy preparing for his upcoming trial. Although he had a lot on his mind, he noticed Ramona had changed. She would sit for hours silently reading her bible. She also spent a lot of time with her pastor either on the phone or at his office. Daryl brushed it off as her just having a deep affiliation with the church and strong devotion to Jesus. He figured she was praying for a miracle, praying her boy would not be found guilty. The one thing he couldn't ignore, though, was the way Ramona would act nervous whenever he mentioned Budda's name. Something was going on with her, and he needed to get to the bottom of it. Even though his attorney instructed him not to associate himself with those who were closely connected to the case, Daryl decided to head upstairs and confront Budda.

He stood in front of the door of Budda's apartment

contemplating for a few seconds. Daryl didn't know how he would react once he saw Budda face to face. After all, it was Budda who gave his name up to the police.

Daryl took a deep breath before knocking on the door. He knew there could be consequences from this confrontation, but he had to get to the bottom of what was going on.

When Budda opened the door, his face turned pale at the sight of Daryl.

"What do you want?" Budda asked, trying to act tough.

"I need to talk to you. Come out into the hallway," Daryl said.

Budda stepped out but kept his door slighty ajar. The strong aroma of haze seeped through the cracks.

"So what's up?" Budda asked as he leaned against the brick wall.

"Why'd you have to go tell the cops about the gun? And while we're on the subject, what's up with you and my mom?"

"The cops had me cornered, son. It was either I tell them the truth or they were gonna charge me as an accessory. I love you, my brotha, but I'm not about to take the rap for you or anybody. You would have done the same," Budda said.

"We partners, man! I thought I could trust you. You knew I couldn't find that gun way before DeeDee was killed! Why didn't you let the detectives know that?" Daryl asked, his anger growing.

"Look, they didn't wanna hear that shit. All they wanted to know was where the gun came from. Anyway, why you so mad? From what I heard, no one's prints were found on the piece," Budda replied matter-of-factly.

"That's not the point. Thanks to you and that bitch Butta Face, I gotta face manslaughter charges! You two just couldn't keep your fuckin' mouths shut."

"Look, don't get mad at me and don't call Butta Face a bitch. She and I are getting kinda serious. I don't appreciate that disrespect, son," Budda replied.

"I don't give a fuck if you're serious with her or not. All I know is that I'm not going to jail for something I didn't do 'cause you and Butta Face have a personal vendetta against me. You know what? Consider our partnership dissolved, son. I can't trust your ass, and I don't want you nowhere near me or my house. Now, before I leave, what did you tell my mom? It's like she can't stand hearing your name."

"Don't look at me," Budda responded. "Your moms and I haven't talked in a minute. You're gonna have to ask her what her beef is."

Daryl wanted to beat Budda senseless. He had a strong feeling Budda had something to hide, but he knew he had to keep cool while out on bail.

"All I'm gonna tell you is stay away from me and my moms. If I find out you even looked her way, I will kill you," Daryl growled before turning his back on Budda.

Budda watched as Daryl made his way to the stairwell door and disappeared.

"You and your bitch mama can kiss my ass," he muttered under his breath before going back inside his apartment and slamming the door behind him.

*****

Daryl spent the following weeks keeping a low profile, only venturing out to see his lawyer or take his mother to church. He also spent time with his baby girl Angel, who had returned to New York to spend time with her daddy. Daryl treasured his days with Angel; she was the love of his life. Every time he rocked her to sleep, he cried silently at the thought of not seeing his little girl again. He was determined to prove his innocence for Angel and Angelina, who he began to think of more as time went by.

Angelina, on the other hand, tried her best to forget Daryl. She heard through the grapevine that he had been released. So, she kept busy with Desire's publishing company, often volunteering to take out-of-town trips to avoid seeing Daryl. Angelina felt a great loss when it came to him. She blamed him for the emotional hell she was going through.

Although Angelina hated Daryl, she did miss Ramona. She had grown attached to her and knew Ramona must have been going through a rough time with Daryl's troubles. She often thought of calling her but was too afraid of Ramona's reaction. One afternoon while packing for her trip to Florida, Angelina fought past her fears and called Ramona, promising herself that she would quickly hang up if Daryl answered the phone. To her relief, she heard Ramona's sweet voice on the other end.

"Hi, Ramona. It's Angelina," she said in a soft tone.

"Angelina! How are you, baby? I've missed you so much," Ramona responded, her excitement evident.

"I'm doing well. I'm sorry if I disturbed you, but I just wanted to know how you were doing. I know it hasn't been easy with all that's happened."

"I'm hanging in there, honey. Daryl's been so worried, though. He's afraid of leaving me and Angel alone if he's found guilty," Ramona told her.

"Well, all we can do is pray for him. Ramona, I want to apologize for my outburst at your home. I was just so hurt by Daryl's betrayal," Angelina stated as she wiped the tears flowing down her cheeks.

"Baby, I understand your pain. What Daryl did to you was terrible. But, I hope with the time that has passed, you have found it in your heart to forgive him. He loves you, Angelina. I do know that."

As much as she wanted to believe Ramona, Angelina couldn't put her heart out there again.

"It's too late, Ramona. If he had any love for me, he destroyed it when he ran around with DeeDee. One thing I do know is that he loves you and Angel. I will pray for him, pray he doesn't end up in prison. Only because I know it would kill him to be apart from you two. But, as for he and I getting back together, it's never going to happen, Ramona. I'm sorry."

"I understand. I didn't get a chance to tell you before, but you have my deepest condolences for the death of your mother, honey. I know she's looking down at you and is happy because of the beautiful woman you have become. By the way, I hear you're doing very well with your new venture."

"Thank you," Angelina replied, smiling. "Yes, I'm happy. I'm actually on my way to Florida to spend some time with my dad."

"Well, you have a great trip. Please feel free to call me anytime. I love you, Angelina," Ramona told her.

"I love you, too, Ramona. I'll call you when I get back," Angelina promised.

After hanging up the phone, Ramona sat on the dining room chair with a look of despair on her face. Then she picked up the bible and cluched it to her chest.

"All has been for nothing," she said softly as she wept.

*****

Two weeks had gone by, and it was almost time for Angel's return to Florida. Wanting to spend as much time with his daughter as possible before she went back to her mother, Daryl decided the two of them would take a drive down south. Bonding with her seemed more important than anything at that point. They left Ramona's house at 7:00 a.m. and drove all day to the southern tip of Virginia, where he checked them into a local motel so they could rest for the evening.

Daryl made it to Tallahassee the following afternoon. He spent the day with Angel before heading back to New York, but before leaving, Daryl gave Katrina thirty thousand dollars. He wanted to make sure his daughter had the things she needed just in case he was sent to prison for a long time.

Alone in his car, he drove all night while smoking haze and thinking of a way to beat his case. Spending time with his child made him more determined than ever to stay out of jail; his innocence would be found in court.

Daryl arrived in front of his building the following afternoon with a renewed sense of hope. The drive home put things into perspective and had him feeling like nothing could stop him from fighting for his freedom. With his child and mother by his side, it's all he needed in the world.

As Daryl approached his front door, the stench coming from inside made his stomach turn. The odor, which smelled like rotting meat, got stronger when he unlocked the door and stepped inside.

"Damn, Mommy, what the hell did you leave out, a whole cow?" he said jokingly while making his way to the kitchen.

But, his lively demeanor turned to worry when he noticed the kitchen was spotless and no meat had been left out on the counter.

Daryl opened the kitchen window and then made his way to the living room. Ramona's knitting kit was neatly placed on the sofa, but there was no sign of her. As he slowly walked towards his mother's room, the stench grew stronger. So strong that he had to take off his t-shirt and place it over his nose and mouth to keep from gagging. After slowly opening the bedroom door, he almost fainted at the sight of his beloved mother lying lifeless on her bed. Her feather-down pillows were soaked in blood and fragments of her brains were splattered on the headboard and nearby wall from an apparent bullet wound to her head. Her wide-open eyes had the look of death.

Daryl frantically called 911 and stayed in the hallway while waiting for the police to arrive. Stunned from the sight of his mother's dead body, he began vomiting uncontrollably. Soon, the police, including Detective Sanchez, arrived at the scene and surrounded the building. After entering the apartment, Detective Sanchez emerged from Ramona's bedroom almost an hour later to talk to Daryl.

"I'm sorry for your loss, son. I know you may not be in the mood for any questions, but I need to know where you were."

"I took my daughter back home to Tallahassee. I left two days ago and just got home today," Daryl replied. Realizing what he had just said, he quickly added, "And my lawyer was aware of my trip."

"Can you give me a number where I can reach your daughter's mother and verify this?" Detective Sanchez asked.

Daryl looked at him with fury in his eyes. "What the fuck? You think I killed my mother?"

"No, I don't. I just need to confirm everyone's whereabouts for the time in question. According to the coroner, it was clearly a suicide. She also left a note for you. I can give you the note to read, but you have to give it back for evidence," Detective Sanchez said as he handed Daryl an open envelope.

Daryl stared at the envelope, afraid to read its contents.

"Look, could you make a copy of it? I have a copier in my room. I can't read it now," Daryl asked, tears filling his eyes.

"Sure, I understand. Look, you can't stay here while the investigation is being conducted. Is there anywhere else you can stay?"

"Yeah, I can stay at my boy Trevor's house," Daryl responded.

"Well, I suggest you leave now. We're gonna be here for a while. Let me get your house keys from you, and you can pick them up at the precinct once we've finished our investigation."

*****

Daryl couldn't remember how he made it to Trevor's house. His mind was in such a fog that he just stepped on the gas pedal and acted as if the truck had an autopilot feature.

All Daryl remembered was calling Trevor while en route and telling him what had happened; everything else was a blur. When he arrived, Trevor quickly whisked him to the basement where a bottle of vodka awaited Daryl, along with a set of clean sheets neatly draped over a futon couch.

Daryl's head was spinning with all kinds of emotions. Anger, pain, and guilt overwhelmed him. He wondered why his mother would take her own life. Sure, Ramona had been acting different after his arrest, but he thought she was just worried about him. He suddenly felt guilty for leaving her alone. He was convinced had he been there she would have never taken her life.

Grabbing the bottle of vodka, his weakened body collapsed onto the futon. He unscrewed the glass bottle, took a big gulp and leaned back, allowing the substance to take over. Daryl then removed the copy of Ramona's letter from his front pocket. Unfolding the note, he began to read:

My Dearest Son, by the time you read this letter, I will be gone. First, let me say that despite all the worry you caused me, I love you with all my heart. Ever since your father died, I tried my best to keep you from choosing the wrong path, but I later realized hustling was in your blood and there was nothing I could do about it.

As a mother, I will do anything to protect my baby. I knew your sister was okay with her father's side of the family, but I also knew you needed extra care.

I took my life because the guilt of what I did overwhelmed me to the point where I was going insane. I will not give further details because I know if I say anything further, this note will not reach you until the detectives have fully done their investigation. I did prepare a separate letter for the detectives, so please see them. It will save your life. I am sorry for any pain I have caused you.

Your Loving Mother,
Ramona

Daryl read the letter a few times, trying to sort out his confused thoughts. He wanted to get to the bottom of it all. As he read the letter for the fourth time, his cell phone rang.

"Who is this?" he answered, irritated with having his thoughts interrupted.

"This is Detective Sanchez. I need to talk to you first thing tomorrow morning."

"And why in the hell should I talk to you?" Daryl barked.

"Daryl, along with the letter addressed to you, there was another letter addressed to me. Come by the precinct tomorrow morning. We need to talk. And bring your lawyer with you."

*****

The next morning, Daryl was at the 32nd Precinct with his attorney and Trevor.

"I'm glad you are all here," Detective Sanchez started as he pulled extra chairs around his desk.

Once everyone was seated, he removed a piece of paper from a folder on his desk.

"Your mother left a second note. It explains why she took her life. The letter contains information important to your case, Daryl. In this letter, there is crucial information about Denise Richardson's murder. Daryl, it's a confession. Your mother killed Denise. She wrote details of the murder not known by anyone outside this precint," Detective Sanchez stated softly.

Daryl shot up from his chair and attempted to lunge at the detective, but Trevor quickly stood in between the two.

"You lying! My mom would never do anything like that!"

The other detectives quickly ran towards Sanchez's desk but stopped once the detective held his hand up.

"It's okay, boys. I'm fine," he assured them.

Mr. Stein sat with a stern expression on his face while adjusting his wire-rimmed glasses. "I need to examine the

155

letter, and I hope you sent a copy to the District Attorney."

Detective Sanchez handed him a copy. "I spoke to the District Attorney this morning and intend to take my findings to his office as soon as I am done here."

The letter explained in detail how DeeDee was killed. Daryl's anguish over DeeDee's pregnancy drove Ramona insane to the point where she went to see DeeDee in an attempt to get her out of Daryl's life once and for all.

*****

Ramona had sent DeeDee a text from Daryl's cell phone asking her to meet on the rooftop of the building where DeeDee lived. She was very careful to erase all of the messages exchanged between them. Once Daryl left for the evening, she went to her bedroom to get one of his guns that she had tucked away in her closet. She discovered the weapons hidden in a sneaker box one day while cleaning his room. At first, she was going to throw the guns away, but for some reason, she thought it would be best to keep them.

Desperate to ease her baby boy's pain, she met with DeeDee and offered her a chance to deliver the child and relinquish all parental rights to Ramona. In return, DeeDee would get twenty-five thousand dollars to go away and never come back. Although Ramona hated DeeDee with a passion, her religious beliefs viewed abortion as a sin. Unfortunately, DeeDee refused her offer.

"You must be crazy, bitch! I put up with too much shit from Daryl to just give my baby to you. Daryl's gonna be mine, and we gonna raise this baby together! As a matter of fact, I'm looking forward to moving into your apartment. Your old ass can go live with your daughter," DeeDee said smugly.

Ramona's flushed face displayed her growing anger.

"Now listen here, you fucking slut! My son DOESN'T want you. You were nothing but a plaything for Daryl and someone who he saw as a convenient fuck. You think he would have intentionally gotten you pregnant?"

"Oh, but it was intentional. It was my intention to get pregnant...and I did!" DeeDee replied sarcastically while rubbing her belly.

Frustrated with DeeDee's attitude, Ramona took the gun out of her purse in an attempt to scare her. However, instead of being afraid, DeeDee laughed and teased Ramona about how she wouldn't dare shoot her, especially with her future grandchild growing inside of her.

As the argument escalated, DeeDee attempted to grab the gun out of Ramona's hand. During the struggle, a single shot rang out and DeeDee fell to the ground. Terrified of what she had done, Ramona tucked the gun in her purse and was about to flee, when the steel door to the stairwell swung open and a young couple stepped out onto the rooftop. Ramona hid trembling in a dark corner until she was convinced they were so engrossed in having sex that they hadn't noticed anything. Ramona then tiptoed to the door, flung the steel door inward, and ran down the stairs as fast as she could until she made her way out the front door of the building. She continued running until she came to the abandoned pier overlooking the East River on 131st Street.

Once at the edge of the river, Ramona's eyes filled with tears as she looked over the dark, murky waters. She first considered jumping into the water. It would have been easy for her to drown and end it all. But, as she was about to lift her leg over the rail, she thought of Daryl and the pain her baby would go through if he lost the only person who was there for him. She couldn't do it to him.

Instead, she nervously grabbed the gun from inside her purse, wiped it clean of her fingerprints, and threw the hardware into the waters, hoping the waves would wash it out into the ocean. As months passed, Ramona felt more confident her son would not be found guilty. The evidence was lost in the ocean below or so she thought. It wasn't until

Ramona got word that the gun had, in fact, been found that her worst fears came to light.

Many times she wanted to walk into the precinct and confess, but she knew she could not bear the pain of having her son see his mother behind bars. It had been difficult enough for her during his seven years of incarceration. She did not want to put him through the same anguish. So, Ramona waited for Daryl to take her grandbaby back home, retrieved Daryl's spare gun, and against her religious beliefs, she took her own life.

*****

"This letter contains information about Leroy Perry, as well," Attorney Stein said as he examined the paper.

"Yes, it does. It seems Budda knew Daryl's mother had killed Denise. The night of the murder, Sandra Anderson, or Butta Face as she's known in the streets, had been standing by the roof's doorway and saw the whole thing. Instead of coming to us, she told Budda, who in turn confronted your mother, blackmailing her to the tune of fifty thousand dollars as written in your mother's suicide note. Armed with a search warrant, we went into Leroy's apartment a few hours ago and took them into custody. They both confessed and will be arraigned for conspiracy to blackmail," Detective Sanchez informed them.

Attorney Stein stood up and placed his hand on Daryl's shoulder. "Mr. James, I will take care of everything. You can go home with your friend, and I will call you when I get back to my office.

Too shaken to answer, Daryl continued to stare down at the tiled floor.

Trevor stepped towards the attorney. "Don't worry, I got him. We'll wait for your call." He then led his friend towards the elevators.

*****

The following week, Daryl stood in front of the judge in criminal court.

"Due to the overwhelming evidence presented in this court, I declare that Mr. James is innocent and is hereby free to go."

And with those words, Daryl was free to leave, but to what? His mother, the only one who had been there for him throughout his life, was not only dead but had taken her life because of him. His mind flooded with memories of his mother sitting on the benches at Marcy Projects where he played on the monkey bars and slides as a child. His mother was an OG; he remembered how she once told him to immediately fall to the floor if he heard gunshots.

"Bullets don't discriminate, boy. They'll hit you whether you're black, white, Asian, grown, or little," she told him.

His sister, Patrice, was of no comfort to him. When she learned of the circumstances surrounding Ramona's suicide, she did not hesitate to blame Daryl.

"It's your fault!" she yelled. "My mom would be alive right now if it weren't for you. I was finally getting to know and love her, and you ruined it with your selfishness. As far as I'm concerned you're just as dead as our mother!"

Those were the last words she uttered before slamming down the phone.

Linda immediately called Angelina after Daryl's court appearance and told her all that had unfolded regarding DeeDee's murder.

"Oh my God, Linda. I can't believe it," Angelina responded.

"Yes, girl. It's like some sort of mystery novel."

It was more than Angelina could handle. There was too much death happening around her, suffocating her to the point of insanity.

"You know, Linda, it's a good thing I promised my dad I

would stay for another month. I can't take all this," Angelina said.

"I know what you mean. It's a lot for all of us to swallow. You have a great time, girl. You deserve it."

*****

That night, Angelina couldn't sleep. The thought of Ramona's lifeless body swirled in her consciousness as she tossed and turned on her plush bed. She remembered the promise she made to call Ramona when she got home. Now that could never be.

The next morning, she awoke to the aroma of honey-glazed bacon. Hungry, Angelina quickly showered and followed the sweet scent that filled her nostrils. She knew who was preparing such a delicious meal.

Doña Rosa was a woman Angelina adored. She was the housekeeper at Nelson's old apartment in New York. Doña Rosa took care of Nelson's children and didn't mind having another mouth to feed whenever Angelina spent time at his house.

Although the kids were grown and out of the house, Nelson's wife made her promise not to leave him when he moved to Florida; she knew Nelson needed her more than she did. So, Doña Rosa gladly went along and became the head housekeeper and gatekeeper of Nelson's mansion. Much older now, her job consisted mainly of overseeing the other housekeepers. Doña Rosa had been on vacation visiting her children in Puerto Rico when Angelina first arrived. Getting back the night before, she promised herself that she would cook a special breakfast for her precious one.

Once in view, Angelina ran towards her, happily wrapping her arms around the old woman.

"Doña Rosa! How are you, ma?"

"Mi niña, I'm okay. A little older, a little wiser and very glad that you are here," she replied.

Angelina could see the tears forming in the older woman's dark brown eyes.

"I'm making your favorite breakfast. I know you miss it, mamita." Doña Rosa then tenderly stroked Angelina's cheek. "I'm so sorry to hear about your mother. You know she loved you very much under the circumstances."

Angelina's eyes filled with tears at the mention of her mother. "I know, Doña Rosa. Did Papi tell you all the details?"

"Yes, he did. Don't worry; you are not to blame for what happened to your mother. She is at peace now," Doña Rosa told her.

"I know, but it still hurts."

"I know, mamita. Listen, I made breakfast and you better eat it. You need your strength. I know you have a lot of work to do," Doña Rosa said with a comforting smile.

"I do have a lot of work, but I am not leaving without eating your world-famous breakfast," Angelina stated as she quickly grabbed a chair.

Doña Rosa did not disappoint. Her eggs and bacon were just what Angelina needed to boost her spirits, and the Spanish coffee was strong enough to revive the dead. Nelson walked in just as Angelina finished the last bit of bacon.

"I see Doña Rosa took care of you well," he commented with a smile.

"Oh yes, she did. I'm so full I can't get out of my chair," Angelina whined while rubbing her belly.

"So do you have to leave right away? There's something I have to discuss with you," Nelson said as he poured the hot, dark liquid into his porcelain cup.

"My appointment isn't until one o'clock, so I have plenty of time," Angelina replied.

"Good. Come with me to the study so we can talk."

As she got up from her chair, Angelina couldn't help but notice the smile vanishing from Doña Rosa's face, but Nelson whisked her away before she could ask her any questions.

161

As they walked towards the study, Nelson began to speak.

"Mamita, you know I would never do anything to harm or hurt you, but there is someone here who needs to speak to you. He's someone who has information you need to know."

Angelina suddenly felt uneasy by his tone of voice.

"Papi, what's going on?" she asked.

"Everything will be revealed once you come inside the study. Trust me."

He led her towards the doors leading to the den. After turning the gold knobs, he stepped back as she cautiously stepped inside.

Angelina noticed a man sitting with his back facing the entrance. She slowly made her way towards him until she was face to face with the stranger. Angelina almost collapsed when she recognized who he was. The gentleman looked up at her and smiled.

"You look as beautiful as the day you were born, my darling daughter," Victor Rivera whispered.

Angelina had to lean against the desk to keep from falling to the floor. The last time she saw her father she was a little girl. A burst of anger stirred inside her as painful memories of his abandonment rushed straight to her head.

"What are you doing here? What do you want?" she exploded.

Victor rose from his chair to embrace her, but she pulled away and ran towards Nelson.

"Papi, why did you let *him* come here? I don't want anything to do with Victor! He abandoned me and my mother!" she yelled.

"Angelina, you know I would never do anything to hurt you, but you need to listen to your father and…"

Hysterical, Angelina didn't let him finish his sentence.

"He is not my father! He's nothing but a sperm donor whose last name I have!"

Nelson grabbed Angelina by her shoulders and lightly shook her to calm her.

162

"Angelina! I know you're angry, but the fact of the matter is that he *is* your father. Now, there is something important we need to discuss. Listen to him."

Exhausted, Angelina took a deep breath and nodded.

"Okay, Papi."

"Good. Let's all sit by the balcony and talk," Nelson said with a smile, trying to ease the tension.

Angelina sat beside Nelson as Victor made himself comfortable across from them.

"Angelina, please believe me when I say not a day went by that I didn't think of you," Victor started.

Angelina sucked her teeth. "Really? And where were you living while you were thinking so much about me?"

"When your mother and I divorced, I moved to the Bronx and then lived in Orlando, Florida, for a while. I moved back to New York when you were eleven years old," Victor responded.

"And in all those years, you didn't bother to see me? Mami lived in the same apartment until the day she died. You couldn't even bother to knock on her door and ask if your daughter was alive or dead?" Angelina asked sternly.

Victor gazed at his daughter with a look of sadness.

"I'm sorry about your mother. I was a terrible husband and father who made your mother's life miserable. I know you have many questions and I promise to answer them. But, right now, I need to discuss with you a matter of grave importance. I need to talk to you about Daryl James.

Chapter 16
Time Doesn't Heal Old Wounds

Daryl's eyes were fixated on the young girl as she seductively wrapped her long legs around the pole in the center of the huge stage. About twenty-one years old, she had long jet-black hair and a voluptuous body that could make a grown man cry. It wasn't her seductive moves that caught Daryl's attention, though. It was her striking resemblance to Angelina that had him glued to his chair.

He hadn't seen Angelina since his initial arrest for DeeDee's murder and found himself missing her badly. Rumors swirled around the neighborhood that she had moved out of Taft Projects, disappearing without a trace. He heard that she lived in the Bronx, but Daryl was never able to get her new address. He tried to get information from Linda, but she always claimed she hadn't heard from her, even though Daryl knew she was lying.

After his mother commited suicide, Daryl decided to leave the book game altogether. He fell into a deep depression, which got worse with every blunt he smoked. Unable to continue staying at his mother's apartment due to the fact that his name was not on the lease, he secured an apartment on Manhattan's upper westside. The quiet, four-story building sat on the corner of Eighth Avenue and 145th Street on a tree-lined street. His window overlooked a children's park, and he would sit there for hours smoking and watching the children play while their mothers and nannies chatted away on the benches. Daryl's depression got so bad that he cut all communications with his child; he didn't want his daughter to see him in such a state.

Daryl would spend his days in Brooklyn tending to his workers as they sold bundles of crack along Marcy Projects. Daryl used his art of persuasion to convince one of the young crackheads that lived in the complex to rent him a room. He had the room's door securely locked and kept his supply in a safe he purchased at the local hardware store. Daryl hit her kitty once in a blue moon to keep her quiet and happy; however, he would get mad whenever she'd tell the locals he was her boyfriend.

He spent his nights at The Drive, a strip club off the Bruckner Expressway located in the South Bronx. There he'd exchange his big bills for stacks of dollar bills and make it rain on the dancers, who would eagerly stuff the paper down their g-strings. Everyone knew he was a washed-up author who now made his money in the drug game, but that didn't matter to them. All they cared about was collecting those dollar bills that would help feed their babies and pay the bills.

But, one particular dancer caught his eye. He saw Angelina in her. With every gyrate of her hips, he remembered how Angelina would put on a show for him when they were together. Daryl brought out the freak in Angelina and he knew it. She was a lady in the streets and a whore in the sheets, just the way he liked it.

The sudden vibration from his cell phone jolted him back to reality. He noticed the unknown number on his caller ID and was about to ignore it, but his gut feeling lured him to answer.

"Yeah, what's up?"

"Mr. James? My name is Anthony Harvey, and I'm the CEO of A.R. Productions. I was introduced to your books by one of our staff members, and I must say your storyline is very interesting. I would like to set up an appointment with you and discuss the possibility of turning your books into movies."

Daryl couldn't believe what he was hearing.

"This ain't no joke, right?" he asked.

"I assure you it's not. I don't joke when it comes to money. Why don't you come by my studio tomorrow night so we could talk about it further?"

"A'ight. What's your address?"

Daryl fumbled around in his pockets looking for a pen. Then he quickly jotted down the address on one of the cocktail napkins and hung up.

"Ladies, this is my lucky night. By this time tomorrow, I'm gonna be a superstar!" he yelled at the top of his lungs while throwing bundles of dollar bills onto the stage.

*****

The next day, Daryl was on cloud nine. He took care of business at Marcy Projects with a renewed spring in his step. If all went well later that evening, he'd soon be walking the red carpet accepting an award instead of stepping into the urine-drenched hallways of the projects. He would finally be able to show his daughter her daddy was somebody.

That evening, he got ready with special care. He decided to wear his black and gray pinstriped suit and gray shirt. He wanted to impress the production company. As he got into his white BMW 328i, which he purchased when he first moved into the small apartment after his mother died, he felt like life was finally dealing him a good hand. No more selling drugs, no more loneliness. He could finally make his money legitimately and maybe find Angelina; he was going to humble himself and beg her for forgiveness for all that he'd done.

He drove over the Williamsburg Bridge and into the southside of Brooklyn. Arriving at Kent Avenue, he felt a bit uneasy with the loneliness surrounding the streets. The warehouse was next to the old Domino's Sugar plant near the Hudson River. Daryl stopped the car and grabbed his .38 special out of the glove compartment, tucking it on his side before continuing to his destination. He arrived at the entrance of the huge warehouse where a stocky Hispanic man sat by the guard's booth. He was a light-skinned man with a shaved head and dressed in black.

"Hey, how you doing? I have an appointment with Anthony Harvey," Daryl told him.

The Hispanic man glared at him for a few seconds before speaking. "Yeah, drive up to Studio B. There's parking right by the entrance."

Daryl quickly found a parking spot. As he got out and made his way towards the door, he didn't notice the shadowy figure creeping up behind him. The last thing he remembered was the pain as the stranger's gun slammed onto his head, knocking him unconscious.

When Daryl came to, he was sitting in the middle of the empty warehouse. His hands and feet were duct-taped to the metal chair. Daryl's head felt like it had been hit with a sledgehammer and the bright lights overhead hurt his eyes. He was able to focus enough to see an empty chair in front of him and three burly guys surrounding it.

"What the fuck is going on?" Daryl asked.

The three guys didn't answer, adding to Daryl's mounting frustration.

"I said, what the fuck is going on?" he yelled.

The burly henchmen stared at him for a second, then laughed. Daryl's frustration turned to fear.

"Look, if it's money you want, I have plenty. I can make sure you guys are set for life. Who paid you to do this? Whatever they're paying you, I will double it," Daryl bartered.

"You can't pay them enough, Daryl. They are loyal to my family."

The familiar voice came from the other end of the

warehouse. As he turned his focus towards the voice, he couldn't believe who was walking towards him. The female figure was almost unrecognizable. She wore leather pants and a bustier. Her long hair was cut short with gelled spikes on top. The heels from her leather thigh-high boots clicked loudly on the concrete floor, echoing throughout the empty room.

"Angelina? What the fuck is going on?" Daryl asked, confused as to what was going on.

As Angelina made her way across to the empty chair, the devilish grin on her face caused chills to travel down his spine.

"How you doing, Daryl? Long time no see," she said, flipping the chair around and straddling it so she could face him.

Daryl's heart pounded so hard he thought it would bust out of his chest. The sudden fear made his head hurt more.

"I'm gonna ask you again, bitch! What's going on?" he growled.

"Oh, we're trying to be tough now? It's funny how you can play tough even though your hands and feet are taped to a chair. But, I guess it's just for show. You must be shitting in your pants right now," she replied with a grin.

"What the fuck is going on!" Daryl yelled.

Unfazed by his anger, Angelina continued.

"I'll explain. You see, six months ago I met my biological father. He told me a story that quite frankly I didn't believe at first until he provided the proof. It's a story on how when he left my mother, he hooked up with a Dominican chick from Brooklyn. She was ten years younger than him and looked hotter than the sun. Her family didn't approve of their union and kicked her out, leaving my dad no choice but to put her up at his crib in the Bronx. His drinking and drugging always caused him to become violent, and like my mom, she endured his constant beatings. He finally quit hitting on her when she informed him that she was pregnant. However, it wasn't long after their child's birth that the beatings continued, and she finally took herself and her little boy back to Brooklyn. Just like my mom, she also raised her child as a single mother."

"What the fuck does that have to do with me?" he asked, his patience wearing thin.

"It has a lot to do with you, my dear. The young boy grew up to become a hustler who partnered up with his childhood friend from the Marcy Projects. The boy unknowingly became friends with one of his customers, who was actually an undercover cop trying to gain his trust. Because of his carelessness, the boy and his partner were caught in a raid and both ended up in prison. The boy's partner blamed him for getting them locked up, and from behind bars, he put a hit on him. A month later, the guards found the boy's lifeless body. He had been stabbed in the chest multiple times," she calmly stated as she glared at Daryl.

Angelina then stood up from the chair and walked towards a stunned Daryl. Towering over him, she grabbed him by his cheeks.

"The young man murdered was Fernando Rivera, my brother. And the bastard who had him killed was Daryl James…YOU!"

Daryl began shaking with fear as tears flowed down his dark cheeks.

"Angelina, I didn't know he was your brother. You gotta understand that I was sent upstate because of him. I had to spend seven years in that prison hellhole because of his stupidity!"

Angelina softened her tone as she stroked the side of his face. "It's okay, Daryl. I didn't know I had a brother until six months ago. But, the fact still remains that you had my brother killed."

Walking a few feet away from him, she stood close to one of the henchmen and whispered something to him. The bald man pulled out a .38 special with silencer attached and handed it to her. She kept her back towards Daryl while holding the gun with both hands.

"First, you broke my heart and used me to further your career. Then you killed my only brother. If it weren't for you, my mother and brother would still be alive, Daryl," she said, tears flowing down her cheeks.

"You can't blame me for those things! I didn't tell you to help me with my book! I didn't know that rat was your brother! And I certainly didn't kill your mother! You did that yourself when your sorry ass got caught drinking and driving. Don't blame me for your fuck-ups, bitch. As far as I'm concerned, I got what I wanted: money, power and respect!" he shouted.

Angelina took a deep breath. "Can you do me a favor, Daryl?" she asked calmly.

"What?" he growled.

His cocky attitude once again turned to fear when she turned around to face him and aimed the gun at his forehead.

"Say hello to my mom, your mom, and my brother for me."

Those were the last words Daryl heard followed by a soft bang. When the smoke cleared, Daryl's brains were splattered on the concrete floor and his lifeless body was slumped over in the steel chair.

Angelina calmly handed the gun to her trusted bodyguard.

"Clean up this mess and get rid of the car," she told them, then walked away into the darkness of the night.

Epilogue

Angelina spent the next two years under the protection of the Cuban government. She lived on the beach in a mansion that her father Victor had purchased years ago far away from the poverty that surrounded the communist country. Victor visited often to check up on his only child, and it was there where Angelina was finally able to get answers to the many questions surrounding her childhood. She learned that her father and Nelson were partners who ran one of the biggest cartels in Miami and New York. They were best friends from high school who worked together for the Italian mob on the eastside of Manhattan until they were given the blessing to go out on their own. Both ran everything from prostitution to illegal numbers in El Barrio, but they were smart enough to keep their jobs at the Housing Authority as a cover until their retirement.

As Nelson flourished in the business, Victor fell victim to the constant women chasing him and soon found himself consuming the same drugs he sold, which caused him to turn violent towards Ana. Once she got the courage to kick him out, he retaliated by cutting all support to Ana and Angelina, leaving Ana to fend for herself with a small child. So, while she struggled to raise a child, the liquor bottle became her only friend. It was a guilt that consumed Victor all of his life.

"Mamita, I hope one day you can forgive me for all I've done to you and your mother," Victor said as they sat on the balcony that overlooked the ocean.

"Dad, I forgave you a long time ago. One thing I've learned is that one cannot change the past, but can use past experiences to make a better future," she told him.

Victor raised his eyebrows and smiled.

"Wow, you just called me Dad."

"Well, it's time I stop calling you by your first name. After all, you are my father," she replied with a comforting smile.

One month after her second year in Cuba, Manolo flew in to visit. He was Nelson's righthand man and had accompanied Angelina when she took care of Daryl. They had become close and secretly became lovers. As the limosine approached the driveway, Angelina ran towards the car in anticipation of seeing her man. She looked lovely in her white form-fitting halter dress and slingback sandals. Angelina flung her arms around her big, burly man when he emerged from the backseat.

"Hi, baby. I'm so glad you're here."

Manolo adored Angelina. He cherished every moment spent with her.

"Hi, mama. I missed you," he said, wrapping his muscular arms around her waist.

Their arms stayed entwined as they walked inside the house and towards the upstairs balcony. The servants had two glasses of mojito waiting on the table outside.

"Mmmm, mojitos. You know how to take care of me, baby." Manolo took a seat on the cushioned lounge chair.

"Only the best for my man," Angelina proudly stated as she nestled next to him.

Both sat silently as they sipped their drinks and watched the sunset dance over the ocean. Halfway through their second drink, Manolo broke the silence.

"Mama, I'm here because your father Nelson sent me to get you. Things in the States have calmed down, so you no longer have to stay here."

"Are you sure?" Angelina asked.

"Yes. Our sources tell us that the cops stopped looking for Daryl. They've closed the case of his disappearance and moved on to the next case," Manolo said, smiling.

"Wow! That's great. I can finally make it to the States and live my life as I please. I can also talk to Papi Nelson and Dad about us."

Manolo laughed. "Too late. I talked to both your dads and both gave me their blessings. I couldn't wait anymore, baby."

Angelina looked into his blue eyes and smiled. "Baby, you're a real man. I'm so glad I met you."

"Me too, baby. Now let's get some rest. We leave tomorrow."

That night, Angelina and Manolo made love under the stars on the private beach. Angelina gave herself to him completely, and he received her with the love and admiration that she had been craving for so long. Finally at peace, she slept in his arms until the sun came up over the horizon.

The next morning, they boarded Nelson's private jet to Miami International Airport. Nelson's connections helped them cut through customs and straight into the limo waiting for them on the tarmac. The limo dropped Manolo off at his home on Miami's Kendall Drive before heading to Orlando. But, Angelina instructed the driver to take a detour towards Sanford.

They drove towards a private school on Laguna Street. She sipped her chardonnay and waited until the school kids filed outside for recess. Her heart raced when she saw one of the students come out of the school doors and join her friends by the palm tree near the fence. It was Angel, Daryl's seed, chatting away with her schoolmates. She looked like a pretty pre-teen in her crisp uniform, although she had her tenth birthday just the month before. Angelina anonymously arranged for Daryl's child to attend private school with all expenses paid by her. She wanted to make sure the child did not turn out like her father.

Satisfied, Angelina instructed the driver to take her to Nelson's house. She arrived to find Nelson and Victor waiting for her at the doorway.

"Welcome home!" they shouted in unison.

Angelina felt good seeing her two dads. For many years, she felt lonely. Now she had more love than she could handle.

"I'm glad to be back," she said.

Doña Rosa prepared a feast of roast pork, rice, and vegetables. They sat at Nelson's spacious dining room table as dish after dish were brought from the busy kitchen and placed before them. Angelina was in heaven.

Once they devoured the huge feast, the trio retired to Nelson's den. Lighting cigars, the two men updated Angelina on what went on during her absence.

"The Daryl case is gone. You don't have to worry," Nelson said.

"Yes, it's gone. So, you can start anew," Victor reassured her.

"I want to thank you both for taking care of things while I was away. You two are the best."

Both men smiled.

"We're here for you," Victor said.

Angelina grabbed a Cuban cigar from Nelson's case and skillfully lit the tobacco before speaking again.

"Now, there's one thing I want to say. I'm sure we can all agree that I've been through a lot and survived. I think I've proven that I am a true player in the game, and I appreciate and respect the empire you've both built. But, I've tasted blood, sweat, and tears…and I only have one request."

Nelson and Victor looked at each other suspiciously and then at Angelina.

"What's the request?" they asked simultaneously.

Angelina took a puff of her cigar. As she slowly exhaled the smoke into the air, she nodded.

"I want in on the family business."

*****

We are taught in church that there is a HEAVEN and HELL.
When we die, we end up in one or the other.
But, after what I've seen and done in my life, I beg to differ.
Yes, there is a HEAVEN, a place of wonderment and joy.
We go there either right after death or 100 years after.
It just depends on what good deeds we've done on EARTH.
Now HELL?
HELL doesn't exist after death. Why not?
'Cause HELL is here on EARTH among the living.
Just ask me how I know!

Angelina Rivera

For bulk and retail sales, please contact:

MCT Publications, LLC
Attention: Maria Hernandez
PO Box 584
New York, NY 10029

Email: mctpublicationsllc@outlook.com

Website: www.mctpublicationsllc.com

Forms of payment accepted:

Business checks or money orders made
payable to MCT Publications, LLC